Even beneath her beauty—mocha-colored skin and mystifying eyes—something inside Rachel James always glowed. But she traded her dreams for love and ended up widowed and alone. Until journalist Ian Beck reminded Rachel of a persistent desire she'd deemed long gone. And his eyes...it was as if they were seeing a woman for the first time. Now, watching Ian and Rachel fight to uncover the truth about Rachel's biological parents—opening doors to secrets and deception—I see her old fears surfacing.

I only hope she doesn't run from the man who's risked his entire career to mend her heart....

Dear Reader,

If you're eagerly anticipating holiday gifts we can start you off on the right foot, with six compelling reads by authors established and new. Consider it a somewhat early Christmas, Chanukah or Kwanzaa present!

The gifting begins with another in *USA TODAY* bestselling author Susan Mallery's DESERT ROGUES series. In *The Sheik and the Virgin Secretary* a spurned assistant decides the only way to get over a soured romance is to start a new one—with her prince of a boss (literally). Crystal Green offers the last installment of MOST LIKELY TO... with *Past Imperfect,* in which we finally learn the identity of the secret benefactor—as well as Rachel James's parentage. Could the two be linked? In *Under the Mistletoe,* Kristin Hardy's next HOLIDAY HEARTS offering, a by-the-book numbers cruncher is determined to liquidate a grand New England hotel...until she meets the handsome hotel manager determined to restore it to its glory days—and capture her heart in the process! Don't miss *Her Special Charm,* next up in Marie Ferrarella's miniseries THE CAMEO. This time the finder of the necklace is a gruff New York police detective—surely he can't be destined to find love with its Southern belle of an owner, can he? In *Diary of a Domestic Goddess* by Elizabeth Harbison, a woman who is close to losing her job, her dream house and her livelihood finds she might be able to keep all three—*if* she can get close to her hotshot new boss who's annoyingly irresistible. And please welcome brand-new author Loralee Lillibridge—her debut book, *Accidental Hero,* features a bad boy come home, this time with scars, an apology—and a determination to win back the woman he left behind!

So celebrate! We wish all the best of everything this holiday season and in the New Year to come.

Happy reading,

Gail Chasan
Senior Editor

Please address questions and book requests to:
Silhouette Reader Service
U.S.: 3010 Walden Ave., P.O. Box 1325, Buffalo, NY 14269
Canadian: P.O. Box 609, Fort Erie, Ont. L2A 5X3

PAST IMPERFECT
CRYSTAL GREEN

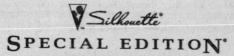

SPECIAL EDITION

Published by Silhouette Books

America's Publisher of Contemporary Romance

Special thanks and acknowledgment are given to Crystal Green for her contribution to the MOST LIKELY TO... series.

Dedication: To Susan Litman, my wonderful editor. Thank you for all the hard work I put you through and for all the talent you've put to good use on my books!

 SILHOUETTE BOOKS

ISBN 0-373-24724-9

PAST IMPERFECT

This edition published by arrangement with Harlequin Books S.A.

® and TM are trademarks of Harlequin Books S.A., used under license. Trademarks indicated with ® are registered in the United States Patent and Trademark Office, the Canadian Trade Marks Office and in other countries.

Visit Silhouette Books at www.eHarlequin.com

Printed in U.S.A.

Books by Crystal Green

Silhouette Special Edition

Beloved Bachelor Dad #1374
*The Pregnant Bride #1440
*His Arch Enemy's Daughter #1455
*The Stranger She Married #1498
*There Goes the Bride #1522
Her Montana Millionaire #1574
*The Black Sheep Heir #1587
The Millionaire's Secret Baby #1668
A Tycoon in Texas #1670
Past Imperfect #1724

*Kane's Crossing

Silhouette Romance

Her Gypsy Prince #1789

Silhouette Bombshell

The Huntress #28

Harlequin Blaze

Playmates #121
Born To Be Bad #179

CRYSTAL GREEN

Crystal Green lives near Las Vegas, Nevada, where she writes for Silhouette Special Edition and Bombshell, plus Harlequin Blaze. She loves to read, overanalyze movies, do yoga and write about her travels and obsessions on her Web site, www.crystal-green.com. There you can read about her trips on Route 66 as well as visits to Japan and Italy.

She'd love to hear from her readers by e-mail through the "Contact Crystal" feature on her Web page!

Dear Rachel,

I'm so sorry you won't be coming back to school next year — but how awesome that you're getting married! I'm so excited for you and can't wait to hear all about your new life with Isaac. Please keep in touch,

XOXOXOXO

Your friend, Cassidy

To Rachel,

We'll all miss seeing you on campus — you brought joy to everyone you met. I wish you all the best luck in your life and marriage. And always remember, if there is anything you need, you can call on me anytime. It has been an honor to have you in my program.

Professor Gilbert Harrison

Chapter One

The man just didn't give up, did he?

Rachel James jogged through a local playground in her west Boston neighborhood, keeping her gaze front and center so as not to make eye contact with the reporter she'd been secretly meeting with for weeks now. While huffing out a cloud of oxygen as her breath met the crisp November afternoon, she concentrated on maintaining her pace, blocking out her frustrations with a cleansing rush of adrenaline.

Still…it was inevitable. Every second brought her closer to Ian Beck, who had his arms draped with arrogant patience over the back of the bench he sat on. Stretching his long, jeans-clad legs in front of him, he

stuffed his hands into the pockets of his leather jacket
and grinned at her.

Even though she tried not to look, she did.

Immediately, a zing of—what was it, more adrenaline?—shot through her. Her belly tied itself into elec-
tric knots.

Butterflies from a brisk jog?

She really didn't want to admit to anything more.

"Gorgeous day for a run," Beck said as she passed
him. "Or another interview."

Instead of answering, Rachel merely held up a hand
in a civil yet discouraging greeting. Wrong time to dog
her with more questions. She was too nervous about tomorrow, dreading what might happen to her good friend
and mentor, Professor Gilbert Harrison, at his board
hearing.

Besides, she'd given the reporter enough information already. As it became more and more obvious
that the university was out to fry Gilbert, Rachel had
taken matters into her own hands by talking to Ian
Beck in private, *without* the knowledge of her friends.
Getting their approval for her "rescue Gilbert" plan
had seemed much too complicated at the time; it
would have been argued and debated to death by committee while Gilbert's situation grew worse. Rachel
had only seen the positives in quietly feeding Ian
Beck good news about her former teacher. So she'd
told him every heartwarming Gilbert anecdote she
could think of. She'd been very vocal about the col-

lege administration's obvious vendetta against everyone's favorite faculty member, and Ian Beck seemed to eat it all up.

And why not? This was scandal at its best: a former English professor and baseball coach fallen from grace, faced with gossip-worthy charges like "grade changing" and "suspicious fraternization with students," among other damning claims. Though the conduct board purported the need to "discover the truth" about the ultrapopular professor, Rachel knew what was really going down. The administration wanted him fired.

No two ways about it.

Loyalty to Gilbert had demanded that Rachel and a group of ex-students accept his plea to return to Saunders University, to stand up for him as character witnesses. A few of them had gone even further, attempting to clear the professor's name by seeking out evidence of the good works he'd accomplished.

But that's when Jane Jackson, Rachel's friend and Gilbert's administrative assistant, had uncovered surprising information about the older man—items that had been locked away in a secret safe. Ledgers featuring cryptic notations. Stacks of highly personal documents about the students he'd helped over the years.

Mysteries.

Jane had delivered one of these personal documents to Rachel without informing Gilbert that it had been taken. For all they knew, he hadn't peered into that safe in months, and they were hoping it would stay that way until they figured out what to do about all the information they'd uncovered.

As Rachel jogged farther away from the reporter, her pace faltered, her mind filled by the image of one particular document that Gilbert had been hiding. A private document that spun her world upside down and made her wonder if she could ever trust him again.

Her very own adoption papers.

Not for the first time—or, she thought, the last—Rachel wondered just what her mentor was up to and why it was his business to have such intimate information about her.

What was he up to? Was he indeed the kind confidant she'd depended on all these years? Or, if he wasn't her trusted friend, then who was he and what did he have up his sleeve?

Measuring her breathing, Rachel expelled another huff and tried to shove the disturbing questions out of her mind. But they only swirled around in there, a screaming flock of discomfort.

Part of the reason she didn't want to talk to Ian Beck today was because she had no idea what she'd tell him about Gilbert now that her adoption papers had been found. Thus, these past few weeks, Rachel had pulled back from the journalist, refusing his requests for more meetings. She was too confused, too shaken by her doubts.

In fact, she couldn't even summon the courage to talk to her once-beloved teacher about any of it.

She rounded a corner, leaping over a pile of dead

burnt-orange leaves that had gathered on the sidewalk. Autumn surrounded her, painting the sky gray, forcing her into sweats, long johns, gloves and a knit cap. As the sound of children playing on a swing set caught her attention, Rachel slowed her speed, grasping the chance to finally get her mind off Gilbert. She softly smiled at the way the mothers hugged their infants, at the way it all seemed so natural for some families....

But before she knew it, there were footsteps hitting the pavement behind her. Another jogger or—

She glanced over her shoulder.

Yes, Beck *was* persistent.

Turning all the way around, she still kept walking, but backward this time, facing the guy head-on even as she moved away from him.

"Listen," she said, gasping for air. Her lungs and skin felt on fire, and she worked off her gloves, stuffing them into her sweat jacket's pocket. "I've got no comments about Gilbert, all right? Shop's closed today."

As he sauntered nearer to her, she was once again lured by the ice-blue of his gaze. He had the face of a handsome pugilist, an old-time fighter you might see in the movies, with eyes that pierced right into their target, a nose slightly flattened by either life or a well-aimed punch from someone who didn't appreciate his tenacity. He wore his brown hair cut short, but his smile was long and slow, the better to draw her in closer for the final punch, my dear.

Since he was panting a little, she guessed that he'd kept pace with her, hoping to catch up.

"Rachel, you've been my best source until now," Ian said. "What's going on?"

He took a step closer, and a flare of that same unwelcome attraction lit through her body, heating her in places that had been laid to rest years ago.

That's the other reason she'd been avoiding him, she thought. Because of the scary nudges of awareness, the sparks of possibility.

She turned around and started to walk off the effects of her jog. It was time to wind it up, anyway.

"Okay," he said. She could hear Ian starting to follow her. "Then I suppose it's not a good time to ask you out for drinks or dinner. Not that you ever accept, anyway."

Boy, she was still heated up. Her skin—the half-black, half-white shade of café au lait that had always made her too self-conscious for her own good—was probably flushed red by now. She flapped a hand in front of her face to cool down, but then realized how counterproductive that was.

He waited out her silence for a moment.

"Is that yet another no?" Ian asked from behind her.

She couldn't help smiling. He was ruthless in his pursuit of a story, and she admired the quality. She'd always wanted to be the same way: Determined. Bulldogged. Steadfast.

Ever since his newspaper, the *National Sun,* had scented a scandal and assigned him to stir up more dirt at the university, the reporter had haunted the area.

Mainly, he was after the former students who'd been asked to come back in order to save Gilbert's reputation—and job. That's why Rachel had chosen to talk to him—because in spite of his paper's recent reputation, his articles hinted at a humanity she hoped might fully sway the public to the professor's side.

"If you're hungry," she said while walking at a quick clip, "go and eat. There's a good Thai place down the street."

"You like Thai?"

This guy really *didn't* give up. "When the mood hits me. But what I'd really like right now is to be left alone. You can respect that, can't you?"

Ian darted in front of her and blocked her progress, hands held out in supplication, that devastating smile sideswiping his lips.

"A brief chat, Rachel," he said. "That's all I'm asking for."

"…said the Wolf to Little Red Riding Hood." Rachel forged ahead, heading home. "I told you. I'm not on the market today."

"Okay. Then what if it *wasn't* an interview?"

He had a glint in his eyes, and Rachel sucked in a breath. Her heart danced, and a tiny pulse in her throat wavered, just like today's fleeting determination to avoid him.

But wasn't that always the case with her? Wasn't her whole life an unlinked chain of joining and quitting, abandoning the promises she'd made?

What a drama queen.

"What are you saying?" she asked Ian.

She stopped in her tracks, and he halted, too. Wind whistled through the trees, fluttering a leaf to the ground beside them.

"Let's just enjoy each other's company." He grinned again, making it seem so easy. "No headlines or quotes involved."

Protectively, Rachel crossed her arms over her chest. "I'm not a big dater, if that's what you're getting at."

He glanced at her bare hand, where her wedding ring would've been if she still wore it. "Why?"

While she searched for an answer, pain winged over her conscience and settled on the edges of instinct, just as it always did when she thought of Isaac.

Not that she had ever talked with Ian about her dead husband, a tender-hearted man with laughing brown eyes, beautiful dark skin and a talent for charming a smile out of anyone.

Ian's voice grew softer. "Would you be insulted if I told you I've done basic research about all my sources? I know that Isaac has been gone for five years now, and you haven't remarried. And as for boyfriends…"

She'd stopped listening, Isaac's name lingering in her mind. A man she'd loved until he'd succumbed to cardiovascular disease and left her much too early.

"Hey." Ian bent down and caught her lowered gaze. Even though the tears didn't come as freely anymore, she still cried every once in a while, especially during cold nights when the rain tapped at her windows and she didn't have anyone to cuddle next to in bed. She missed waking up in the morning to find him reading the paper at the kitchen table, missed how he'd come home from his construction work to wrap her in a bear hug. Missed the unconditional love she'd been craving her whole life—something she'd never really felt from the African-American parents who'd adopted her.

All in all, she guessed she missed the knowledge that he'd always be there for her. It clawed at her to know that she'd already gotten her big chance for love and it was gone for the rest of her days. After all, who found that sort of connection twice in a lifetime?

"Everything's okay." Rachel glanced up at Ian again. "But I don't date much. I'm…too busy, you know?"

The journalist nodded, but she couldn't say he was convinced. He still had a knowing look about him. "I'm up on your schedule. Three days a week working for Nate Williams as a paralegal. The rest of the time you're helping the professor by rounding up evidence…. Check that. You *were* helping the professor."

Rachel swallowed at the mention of it. So he'd noticed the way she'd pulled away from Gilbert. You couldn't fool someone who made a living digging into places his nose didn't belong.

As she started walking again, Ian fell into step with her. He was tall enough so that she had to lift her head to steal a peek at his face, but he wasn't *too* tall.

Good kissing height, she thought, her lips tingling as she glanced at his mouth.

She saw him forming more words, heard them through her filter of loneliness and yearning.

"I noticed," he said, "that lately you haven't been very social with your friends, either, Rachel."

"Told you." She tore her gaze away from him and focused on the steamed window of a bakery, pastries and cakes decorating the display. "I've been busy."

Oddly accepting, Ian merely nodded. Had he somehow gotten wind of what her friends were saying about her? Fellow Gilbert-admirers such as Sandra and David Westport who often asked her why she'd recently retreated into herself?

The adoption documents. The secrets of her life held in a safe.

As she and Ian continued moving past the boutiques and bookstores, she thought of all the rumors constantly circulating around Gilbert—questions about his relationships with some students, speculations about the tone of his friendly office meetings where the kids would hang out to shoot the breeze and get a good dose of optimism and counseling.

Dammit, Rachel thought. She should know better when it came to her mentor. He'd been nothing but caring and supportive with her, so how could she doubt him so much now?

She and Ian approached the Thai restaurant, and he slowed down, jerking his head toward the entrance.

"Come on," he said. "Just a snack."

Rachel brushed a hand over her flat belly. She'd grown up listening to parents who'd told her that she wasn't worth the food they fed her, so, more often than not, she'd gone without the extras.

It was a pattern, she thought. Something to cling to.

"I'm not really hungry," she said, even though her stomach was a little flitty. But maybe that wasn't because of the lack of grub.

Maybe it was a different kind of hunger altogether. Her heart thudded once again. *Ian Beck.*

Pure junk food.

"Don't give me excuses," he said, tugging on her jacket. "Let's go inside. It'll be warmer."

She protested, but he wasn't listening. No, instead she found herself easily giving in—yeah, like she put up a real fight—and followed him down a small stairway into the spicy aromas of the restaurant. Five tables clustered around a bar, where a lit menu offered dishes such as *panaeng nuea* and *tom yam goong*.

He got the *pad thai* and turned to her expectantly, blue eyes shining. "You like it hot?"

Somehow, she got the feeling he was referring to more than food. Her face flushed, and she returned his saucy grin. Heck, why not? Miss Popularity—that was her. But, honestly, she was tired of fretting and could actually use a laugh with the reporter—even if she was dangerously close to flirting with him.

"I'm really not in the mood for anything heavy," she

said, hoping he understood her meaning on more than one level. Then she spoke to the counterperson. "Just an iced tea and a glass of water, please."

"Oooh. Push that envelope." Ian dug in his back pocket for a wallet, producing several bills that would cover the total.

Rachel told him that she didn't have any money on her, and Ian answered that it was his treat. Still, she knew she wouldn't have been able to afford even this tiny bonus splurge on her budget, anyway. Ever since Isaac had fallen ill, she'd been burdened with financial troubles. It had even gotten to the point where she was ready to sell her home to pay all the outstanding medical bills. Thank God for her boss, Nate Williams, who had worked up a payment schedule when she'd refused his offer of assistance. Thank God for Gilbert, too, because he'd mailed her small loans on occasion over the years, even if the two of them hadn't been as close as they'd been during her college days.

Before she'd let him down by dropping out.

Consequently, she swore she'd pay Gilbert back once she lifted herself up again, swore she'd become the type of person who could handle life on her own, even if it killed her. She would've liked to have accomplished this by her thirtieth birthday, but even *that* had passed by without success.

But what was new?

Ian retrieved a plastic marker with their order number on it and led Rachel to a table by the high window. Here, the two of them could see everyone's feet as they walked by on the sidewalk: Ugg boots, business shoes, high-fashioned heels and Timberlands, just like the ones he wore.

With a flippant exhalation, he leaned back in his chair, stretching out his legs again, showcasing his boots as he ran a hand through his hair, leaving it sticking up.

"So, Spike," she said, gesturing to his careless coif, "this is it, then? We're just hanging out, getting heartburn, oohing and aahing over noodles?"

"If you were eating anything, I'd be all for it." He flashed another smile at her, and a slow beat of silence fluttered between them.

"What?" she asked, fidgeting, taking off her knit cap and adjusting her hair. It fell down to her shoulders in the usual tangle of dark curls.

"I'm just…" Ian leaned forward, lowering his voice. "I'm wondering about you, Rachel James. I can't quite figure you out yet, and that's pretty rare."

"Do more research." She smiled at the waitress who set the beverages and food on the table.

"Don't worry, I'll get to more than the basics about this whole story." Ian dug into his meal as soon as the waitress left. Plastic fork halfway to his mouth, he said, "As far as *you* go, though, I know about Isaac, obviously. And your job and schedule, because I like to keep tabs on where my sources are when I need them."

Wow, how heady, she thought as she downed most of her water. *I'm his source, in spite of this incredibly intimate snack break and everything.*

Not exactly a heart-pounding, fantasy-inducing revelation.

But it was better this way, business-only. Right?

While Ian stuffed noodles into his mouth, Rachel finished her water and began to sip her tea. It was thick and sweet, laden with cubes of ice.

Funny how they didn't have much to talk about when he wasn't trying to get a headline out of her. Was now a good time to get personal? Even at first sight, she'd wondered about the details of him: the way one ear was slightly higher than the other, the scuffs on his leather jacket, the been-there-done-that shade of his gaze. The occasional shadow that passed over his eyes during their interviews.

But…no. She didn't have the gumption.

Instead, to cover the awkward pauses in conversation, she resorted to babbling, even though she'd made it clear that she didn't want to talk about the hearings. But Gilbert was all they had in common, and it beat not talking at all, she supposed.

Still, in the back of her mind, she wondered if he was working his reporter mojo on her, even though her wariness didn't stop her mouth from moving.

"So tell me," she said, "when is that first article coming out?"

He washed down his food with the beer he'd ordered, then said, "My editor wants to start the series this coming Monday. It won't be news so much as a column chronicling how the hearing affects the community.

Each following installment will cover what happened the day before and—"

"And how the proceedings stir up the drama and mayhem with all the tawdry details. Jeez. That's why I agreed to talk to you in the first place, Ian, because Gilbert doesn't need theatrics. I'm doing damage control and trying to spread the good word about him."

"Hey." He set down his glass bottle. "I'll be respectful of the situation."

She considered the articles she'd recently seen in his paper and didn't respond. He seemed to read her mind.

"Did it ever occur to you that, unlike the others, I'm not into the muckraking business?"

"Yes. But lately your paper is."

A muscle in his jaw constricted. So did his fingers as they wrapped around the beer bottle. He seemed to be fighting himself about something. Those shadows in his gaze told her as much.

But just as soon as the emotion had appeared, it evaporated. He dug his fork into his noodles again, carefree as ever. "I report the facts as I see them, that's all."

"And how do you see them in this case?"

He paused, set down his fork, grinned. Yet this was no ordinary Beck-smile. No, this was partially feral, a twist on his charming act.

Rachel's breath caught in her chest, but she still held his stare. She'd spent a lifetime backing down, backing away. And she was *done* with it.

Even so, she had the nagging feeling that, as soon as she left Ian, she'd go right back to hiding, ducking confrontation. Odd how she was empowered to stand up for herself only when she was around this particular guy. Somehow, he seemed to nonchalantly encourage her, bringing out what little strength she had.

In fact, it seemed that he rather enjoyed getting a rise out of her.

"I see it this way," he said. "The administration believes that your Gilbert is 'old fashioned' and behind the times. They say he's too much of a friend to the students, and would love to replace him with someone new."

"Is that what you believe?"

"I don't have the luxury of believing anything." Ian rested his arms on the table, still dangerous. "As I said, I only report the facts."

"You know those aren't facts at all."

"Who can be sure? That's why there's going to be a hearing tomorrow."

"Hearing. Huh." Even though things weren't going smoothly with Gilbert right now, Rachel rose to the occasion, paying her mentor back for everything he'd done over the years, protecting him from the bottom of her heart. "It's more like a witch hunt. Surely you've found that the administration has an agenda."

For a spine-tingling moment, Ian's gaze blasted into her. A hunter's eyes.

Then he sat back again, apparently satisfied. "Smart

man, that Gilbert, calling on the right people to defend him. All his favorite students from the past."

"Not just 'students,' Ian. You've seen the list. Nate, our notorious defense lawyer. Kathryn, who was a model before that awful car accident. Jacob, an esteemed fertility specialist… Should I continue? Because I can."

He took her bait, highly engaged by the fire he'd lit under her. "Please do."

"An assistant to an ambassador— You know, it's not going to be hard to show that Gilbert produced success in our own lives *and* for the world at large. The board is going to come off badly when we're done with it…."

She stopped, suddenly aware that she wasn't one of those successes she'd listed. She'd left Saunders during her junior year to marry Isaac, and it'd broken Gilbert's heart. He'd bemoaned the education she was deserting, reminded her that she was just leaving before she could finish what she'd started. Truthfully, Rachel had suspected there'd been more to it than that. That her mentor had been grieving the loss of their relationship, knowing it would never be the same once she married and put Saunders behind.

Ian was watching her, a sympathetic light in his eyes. God, no wonder he was so damned good at getting his story. He really knew how to work his subject.

"It must've been hard," he said, voice soft.

She stared at her tea. The creamy shade of brown reflected everything she'd hidden from all her life. The color of mixed skin that never quite belonged, a tint that had set her apart from family and community.

"What's hard?" she asked.

"Coming back to find Gilbert, seeing he's changed from the energetic, positive man you used to know."

Gilbert. Because of his plea to return to Saunders for this hearing—and her great need to make up for all the disappointment she'd caused him—Rachel had seen him in person for the first time in months. Usually, they caught up with each other over the phone, but that hadn't prepared her for the light that had gone out of his gaze, the wrinkles that had invaded his once-firm skin. But what hurt the most was seeing those proud shoulders slumped under the weight of all these heinous accusations. He'd been protecting so much, she thought, especially when it came to the biggest secret of all—his status as an anonymous benefactor who'd helped so many students during their worst days. Only one of the few who knew about this, Rachel was straining to stay silent, to make Gilbert believe that she and most of her other friends didn't know about this bombshell.

Now, Rachel nodded to Ian, unable to deny the shock of Gilbert's recently degraded appearance, the sadness of her friends who also loved the professor.

"Yes," she said, voice choked, "it was hard seeing him this way. But that's why we're back, to bring him around again. Just like he did for us."

"And just like someone else did," Ian added.

Rachel froze while he eased out his notepad.

She should've seen this coming, but she wasn't as good as this pro. He'd definitely been doing his research.

"Rumor has it," he said, "that there's been an anonymous benefactor who's helped select students on campus for many years at their moment of greatest need. And guess what?" Ian offered her yet another cocky grin.

She stared straight ahead, giving nothing away.

"Those students just happen to include most of your friends," Ian added. "Any comment?"

Chapter Two

Even the next morning, as Ian strolled over one of the manicured lawns that covered the Saunders campus, he couldn't believe he'd been so blunt with Rachel James.

Kid gloves, he reminded himself. This particular woman required a little more finesse than most.

When he'd busted right out with that benefactor query, he'd been going for the shock effect, the pure second of truth in an interviewee's eyes as he or she absorbed the question. Rachel hadn't been any different than the other countless subjects Ian had ambushed for a story—it was just that her unguarded reaction had gotten to him this time. She had bent his heart as if it were heated steel, reshaping it until his pulse had finally cooled hours later.

It bothered him to be treating Rachel James like another cog in the wheel of his career, and this shocked Ian, a man who wasn't so used to regret.

In fact, her reaction had caused him to really look at himself in the mirror this morning…and he didn't like what had peered back at him: a man with the flint of self-loathing in his gaze.

Maybe he just felt bad about the way she'd left the little Thai restaurant without another word to him, slipping on her knit cap and walking out of the place with a dignity Ian could only wish for. Or maybe he was getting soft in his skills, just as his new editor had muttered last week.

Remorse. Emotional second-guessing. Hell, his job didn't allow him those sorts of perks. Nope. His profession—damn, that was sure a noble word for digging up crud and slinging it over a page just to make a buck—demanded that he chase Rachel down again.

Yet, frankly, he had the sneaking suspicion that she knew something about the "mysterious benefactor" of Saunders University, so he had every reason to pursue the matter, anyway.

A looming clock tower struck eight times, the bells ringing through the cool air. Ian fixed his gaze on Lumley Hall, the maple-shrouded red-brick building where Professor Gilbert Harrison's hearing would be held. Students wearing scarves and nosy frowns were loitering outside, and Ian's reporter sense prodded him to ask a few questions, just to establish the tone for today's proceedings.

Were these kids here to support the professor? Or did they, like the administration, have an ax to grind?

Somehow Ian doubted they did, based on the information he'd gotten so far. Everyone seemed to love Gilbert Harrison—except for the old stodgies in charge.

While passing one of many bike racks that dotted the campus, Ian scanned the crowds again, locking in on a single person who stood outside of the hall.

Rachel James, the one-time queen of the campus.

Although she was clearly included in a cluster of friends, she was standing on the fringes, arms crossed over a long, camel-colored coat that had seen better days. Her black hair fell to her shoulders in a cloud of rough curls, and she had a wool scarf wrapped over the bottom half of her face, hiding the full lips Ian had entertained more than a few wicked thoughts about.

He took a couple of seconds to appreciate her, this serene woman who obviously had so much more going on beneath the surface than she would reveal. He could tell by the troubled depths of her almond-shaped brown eyes, by the way they often reflected a level of sadness that he wanted to understand.

Damn, he thought, ambling closer to her. It was all pretty interesting, this new side he was discovering about himself. He didn't really stick around women long enough to develop anything beyond the superficial warmth of a morning-after glow, not that his job allowed him to do more than that, anyway. Still, he always seemed to find willing-enough partners who understood what they were both getting into.

Would a woman like Rachel James...?

What? Agree to eat local cuisine, drink some wine and come back to his hotel every night until he checked out and moved on to the next assignment, the next affair? Not likely. Not someone sweet and earthy like her.

It didn't matter, though. She was only a misguided tickle to his sex drive, encouraged by any number of things: the slam-in-the-gut rush of the first time he'd identified his beautiful source on campus and talked with her, going beyond their all business phone conversations. The willingness she'd shown to talk to him further—albeit secretly—even though her friends weren't nearly so accommodating. The way she watched him— as if she expected mcre of him than muckraking.

How could one assessing look from her make him reevaluate the growing compromises of his job, the sleazy need to uncover scandal, the negativity that his editor emphasized more every week?

Wiping away a twinge of guilt that was recurring far too much lately, Ian boldly approached Rachel, donning his give-me-some-info facade once again: the persuasive smile, the relaxed frame of his body.

"Morning," he said, nodding at her, then at all her friends.

They gave him an assessing glance, said hello, then discreetly—and not rudely—huddled into themselves, closing their circle against him.

But Rachel didn't step into it. Instead, she tugged the scarf off her face and subtly gestured to a spot beneath a lone oak tree, indicating with an angry gaze that he should meet her there.

Well, he thought. *Looks like she's still a bit put out by yesterday's impromptu interview.*

A thrust of desire heated Ian's belly as he followed in the wake of her jasmine perfume. She had his libido's number, with that smooth, light brown complexion, those long eyebrows winging over dark, liquid eyes, those high cheekbones and lush mouth. Even though she had the delicate features of an exotic pixie, he could sense a woman's blood—hot and alive—pulsing under her skin.

"What are you doing?" she asked.

He glanced around, as if flummoxed. "I heard there's a trial going on."

"A closed trial."

Ian's journalistic ambition kicked awake. "Not according to the president of the college board of directors. Alex Broadstreet invited the press."

She merely stared at him for a moment. Her eyes resembled open wounds that bled dark frustration.

His first instinct was to touch her, to let her know that she'd get through this all right. But Ian checked his guts, reminding himself that he'd only be asking for trouble.

"Broadstreet can't do that," she finally said. "He can't bring a private hearing to the public."

Ian made a mental note to get hold of the campus's

conduct-hearing guidelines. But since Broadstreet was the Grand Poo-Bah in charge, Ian suspected he could mold the rules to his own advantage pretty easily.

When Ian glanced at her again, the pain hadn't gone away. It was too much to stand.

"Rachel." He battled with himself, then reached out to casually tug on the lapel of her coat, thinking it wasn't much of a come-on and, therefore, nothing to worry about. "Broadstreet *is* doing it, whether you like it or not."

"Damn him." She huffed out an exasperated breath, then absently caressed the patch of worn wool he'd touched. "He's bound and determined to do anything to disgrace Gilbert. This isn't right."

For a moment, neither of them spoke. She was still holding the tips of her fingers against the material, her head tilted, eyes wide with so many questions he couldn't answer. It was as if, among other things, he'd bewildered her with his halfway playful gesture.

Strangely embarrassed for some reason, Ian took a step back.

Out of self-preservation, he once again assumed the role of unbiased reporter, even though there was a niggling poke of ethics in his gut that was agreeing with Rachel.

In an effort to fully distance himself, he said, "Can I quote you on your disgust regarding the hearing's parameters?"

He couldn't have chosen a colder thing to say.

She shot him a look—the kind every man feels sorry about receiving—then started walking back to her friends. It wasn't as if he hadn't grown used to this sort of reaction. In his line of work, he didn't exactly endear himself to people.

So why did this particular brush-off sting?

He watched as she situated herself in back of Jane Jackson, Gilbert's secretary. Next to Jane stood her fiancé, Smith Parker, a campus maintenance worker. Ian suspected that the two, along with Rachel and Sandra Westport, had investigated Gilbert's situation themselves on the quiet.

As Rachel whispered into the redheaded Jane's ear, Ian was interrupted by the arrival of Joe his photographer.

"Ready to do some damage?" asked the short, squat shutterbug.

Ian tried not to flinch, especially with Rachel standing only yards away. Somehow, she made him too conscious of what his editor had instructed him to do: sell more papers with salacious details.

"If damage involves the truth," he said through a clenched jaw, "then I want it."

Joe chuffed and shifted his cargo. "You're talking like we're back in the golden days of journalism, Beck. Remember, the *Sun* don't report actual news much now. We're in to…what does the boss call it? Titillation. Red ink. *Dirt*."

Once again, the term *tabloid* stabbed at Ian, even

though his newspaper had ridden the coattails of a more prestigious reputation for the last few years. But that's all it was—a reputation that was slowly crumbling with the addition of what the new editor called "selling points."

Ian gestured toward the growing throng of students who were waiting outside the hall. "Joe, let's start off by taking the temperature over there, then we'll set up inside."

"Will do."

And, as Ian Beck went about his work, he tried to avoid Rachel's gaze, which had settled on him like an invisible hand that was guiding him away from the demands of his job and toward something that resembled ethics.

A hand that a fly-by-night reporter like him had been spending way too much energy trying to dodge lately.

"Earth to Rachel?"

She whipped her attention away from the retreating Ian Beck and focused on Jane Jackson, whose pale green eyes were narrowed in speculation.

With an innocent smile, Rachel controlled the thrum of her heartbeat, then focused on a man who was speaking decisively into a cell phone. Nate Williams, her boss and fellow Saunders alumni.

An attorney who was on fire with the news Rachel had just given him.

"I need access to the Saunders board's hearing guidelines," he was saying. "I'll be back in the office after Katie's testimony, so have everything ready for me to tear Broadstreet a new... Yeah, you've got it. Thank you."

Rachel knew that he was having one of the paralegals do the grunt work. Normally, Nate depended on her to be his right hand, but since they were both involved in the hearing and she had rearranged her days off to be here, that was impossible.

As he ended the call, he grumbled, "It's not bad enough that Broadstreet scheduled this on a Friday, knowing the hearing would go for more than one day and Gilbert would have to stew over the weekend. Now he has to invite the world. Bastard."

His girlfriend, Kathryn Price, a former model whose incandescence wasn't at all marred by scarring from an awful accident, laid a comforting hand on Nate's arm. The powerful lawyer, so revered in the courtroom, practically melted under her gentle touch.

Rachel had to glance away, deeply affected by the sight. Once upon a time, she'd had love, too, and she knew how easily it could disappear, stranding you.

"Rachel?" Jane repeated her name. "Kind of distracted today, huh? But...what am I saying? You've been a walking zombie lately."

Pulling her coat tighter around her body, Rachel anticipated Jane's next question, which would no doubt contain the words *what* and *is* and *wrong*.

"I just wish Gilbert would get here," she said, finding a decent explanation for her spaciness. "I want this hearing to be done and over with."

"Don't we all." Jane paused, then jerked her chin toward Ian Beck, who was mingling with the students over by the hall's entrance, chatting them up. "You and the reporter were having some kind of exchange back there."

Rachel shrugged, trying to play it cool, to deny her association with Ian. "He was getting my reaction the news about Alex Broadstreet and how he's found yet another way to mess with Gilbert. That's all."

"Oh." Jane paused. "I thought maybe it was something else. You know, like hormones."

"Jane." Rachel didn't mean to sound like a first-grade teacher talking to a kid who was about to dump a bottle of finger paint onto the table, but she had to dispel *that* notion before it got out of hand. "He's just doing his job. That's it."

"Ri-ight."

"Don't give me that grin. I'm serious."

"Of course you are. When he touched your coat and gave you that hot look, it was *all* business."

Hunger waved down Rachel's body, even as she searched for a comeback. But, thankfully, the conversation was cut short by the arrival of Sandra and David Westport.

The ex-athlete and his blond, blue-eyed wife, a local reporter in her north end neighborhood, hugged Rachel in greeting, as if she were a prodigal child they hadn't seen for years. Silly, really, because she'd just run into them on campus the other day. Granted, she'd made an excuse to leave right away, but it wasn't like she was…

Okay, yeah. She was avoiding them. Those adoption papers from Gilbert's safe had thrown Rachel into a tailspin, jetting her back into the confusion of her youth—a time when her adoptive parents had made her feel so isolated, so confused. A time when she'd been taught that retreat was the safest option.

And now with Ian Beck asking questions about the benefactor…

Sandra kept her arm around Rachel's shoulders. Was her friend restraining her in case she ran away again?

"We were thinking," Sandra said, "that, after the hearing, some of us would go down to Brewster's for a recap."

"Or a nightcap," David, her husband, added.

Jane smiled. "Or, in our case, it'll be an afternoon cap."

The attempted joke made them laugh softly, but the sound was stilted, colored by the anxiety they were all feeling for Gilbert. Rachel had already told Jane about Ian's benefactor queries, and she knew that this tavern meeting would just be another group discussion about what to do with their secret information regarding Gilbert. As usual, the meeting would go nowhere, because no one wanted to pile more stress on their mentor by revealing what they knew. In fact, the gang would probably spend more time asking Rachel what was wrong than anything else.

So why should she go?

Instinctively, Rachel patted Sandra's arm and started to remove herself. "I can't. I'm..."

Before she could say "Busy," she saw the looks on everyone's faces. The traded I-told-you-she'd-refuse glances.

She didn't bother to finish the excuse.

Instead, she changed the subject. "Where's the rest of the crowd?"

David glanced at his watch. "Jacob and Ella are running late because of the little bun in the oven, but they'll be here. Eric and Cassidy are bringing Gilbert. They went over to his place early, just to steady him."

Biting her lip, Rachel held back a rush of sorrow. She should have been the one who volunteered to drive him, to perk him up.

And from the way everyone was watching her, Rachel knew that *they* knew it, too. Knew that they were all dying to ask her what had happened to make her so standoffish.

Only you and I know, Rosemary, she thought, addressing the woman whose name had been burned into Rachel's memory. The name of a woman Gilbert, the benefactor, had no doubt helped along the way, too.

Rosemary Johnson, her birth mother, a woman Rachel had never known. Was she dead? Alive? All Rachel wanted was to find out more about the mysterious lady, even if she might not like what she discovered. But she didn't have the courage. How could she when

Rosemary had deserted her in the first place? And what about the empty spot on those papers, the glaring space where her birth father's name should have been?

Rachel could imagine the worst—Rosemary, single and pregnant, relieved to give up the unwanted baby that had been forced upon her. It wasn't as if finding Rosemary and learning the truth was going to bring happiness to Rachel's life.

Right?

For the next few minutes, everyone made small talk, giving Rachel peace. Then Eric Barnes and Cassidy Maxwell arrived, holding hands as they followed Gilbert.

Professor Harrison, neatly dressed in a long tweed coat and scarf, was accepting a lot of love from the young students who flanked him, students who adored him as much as Rachel did.

Students who were still fresh-faced and eager to listen to all his advice.

For a second, Rachel saw him as the man he used to be: filled with enthusiasm and pep, his brown eyes sparkling with wit and affection. But then he glanced over at her, and she saw the reality: the bent shoulders, the gray in his hair, the fading energy.

Still, Rachel's emotions overwhelmed her, bringing a brilliant smile to her face as she chanced a wave at her beloved mentor.

He brightened at this, and she realized how much she affected him, how happy she made him when she was around.

Yet she'd always known that, ever since the day she'd quit college and he'd practically begged her to come back.

Just as she was about to take her first hesitant step toward Gilbert, the press surrounded him. In their ranks she saw Ian Beck, his pen poised above his notebook as he observed Rachel.

She could tell he knew that she was hanging back, too riddled with doubts to go to Gilbert.

Turning aside from the journalist's measuring gaze, she entered Lumley Hall with her friends, feeling as if they were about to step into a fighting ring.

The spacious lecture hall was filled with observers and echoing with Alex Broadstreet's voice as he spoke into the standing microphone. He was reading the board's charges against Professor Gilbert Harrison, his tone as rich and full of crap as a senator on the campaign trail.

Ian was tuning the man out because he was more than familiar with Broadstreet's complaints. Instead, he inspected the faces.

That's where the real story was—in the people, not the unproved speculations.

Next to him, Joe took another picture of Broadstreet's grandstanding. The flash caught a real headline moment, the spit-polished president pointing his finger in the air, his brows raised in righteous indignation.

Broadstreet was forty-two, sleek as a political ma-

chine, smooth and polished in a creased gray suit. From
the get-go, Ian had gotten a bad vibe from him, and he
trusted his instinct implicitly. It had served him well
over the years in every hard-hitting assignment from
Bosnia to Iran, from Sudan to the urban ghettos of
America. But those had been the days of real news, and
sometimes Ian feared that he'd lost his edge during recent stories like this one, where the intention was to
shock instead of illuminate.

As the president gabbed on, Ian took another opportunity to peek at Rachel James, who had a front-
row seat along with the rest of her friends. Late
arrivals Dr. Jacob Weber and Ella Gardner had
sneaked into their nearby seats just moments ago, giving Ian an excuse to train unfettered attention in
Rachel's direction.

But it was almost as if she was stridently avoiding
him. Was it because she was questioning his part in the
proceedings?

Hell, he couldn't blame her.

The audience stirred as Broadstreet called David
Westport as the first character witness for Gilbert, then
retreated to his seat behind a long table. He was surrounded by the nine other faculty members and ten students who composed the board.

The people who would be deciding Gilbert's fate.

At the other end of the table, Professor Harrison sat
by himself. Ian noticed that the older man kept glancing at Rachel, as if measuring something about her.

There was a real story somewhere. Beneath all the dirt, there was definitely something else blooming.

By now, David Westport had taken his place at the other end of the table. A former college jock, he looked daunting with his flashing green eyes, coal-black hair and all-pro shoulders. As he sat, he sent Broadstreet a glare of pure distaste—not that it fazed the president—then turned the tables and winked at Gilbert.

Cameras flashed, causing Ian to once again notice how much of a circus Broadstreet had constructed. The president really had something against Gilbert, and from what Ian knew, he suspected it all had to do with running the college like a dictator.

And a lot to do with personal jealousy.

For the next half hour, Broadstreet allowed the witness to praise Gilbert, to expound on the professor's exemplary guidance skills and giving nature. It was a good start.

Until the president dove in.

"Mr. Westport," he began, "thank you for the testimonial."

"Anything for Professor Harrison," David said, smiling.

"Yes. Yes, you know, that seems to be our problem." Broadstreet shuffled some papers while clearing his throat. "Or, should I say, the professor's willingness to do anything for his *students* is the real sticking point."

From the very first, Ian had been bowled over by the sense of loyalty Gilbert inspired in his students, former and present. Now, as his attention drifted to the professor—a beaten version of the savior he was supposed to be—Ian's heart actually went out to him. Quickly, he sketched the older man in his notepad, wanting to capture the weariness, the lines of exhaustion mapping his face.

Then, it got ugly.

Broadstreet began questioning David Westport about his poor high school grades, clearly catching the big guy off guard in light of how the proceedings had been going so far. It seemed that, in spite of his academic woes, Westport had received an athletic scholarship, and the president hounded him on how this could've possibly happened.

During all of this, Ian kept glancing at Rachel, noting how pained and baffled she appeared.

There's something deeper going on in her head, Ian thought. Something that was rooted below Westport's academic record.

And as Broadstreet revealed that Gilbert Harrison had been instrumental in securing this scholarship for David Westport, the hall was silenced.

Temporarily victorious, the president turned to Gilbert. "What's your response to this, Harrison?"

The audience stirred, clearly noticing how Broadstreet had already stripped Gilbert of his title.

The older man sighed, offering a weary smile and spreading out his hands. "I have no comment, other than to say that even if David seemed to be an undeserving candidate for the scholarship, he's since proved his worthiness."

He wasn't directly defending himself? Why?

Without thinking, Ian scribbled notes. Westport had worked with kids after college, strengthening their self-esteem through the creation of a sports camp. Maybe that was all the defense Gilbert thought he needed.

As if to prove that theory, a smattering of light applause came from the crowd at the mention of Westport's eventual success, but Broadstreet held up a hand, silencing them.

The president went on from there, hardly cowed.

He ripped into Professor Harrison, saying that there was no way of knowing whether or not Westport was worthy of the scholarship, seeing as no one could've foretold the future back then.

All the while, Gilbert Harrison refused to defend himself further.

With a flurry of penmanship, Ian wrote, "Why the refusal to answer?"

After that, the president went on to attack Gilbert, painting a picture of a scheming professor who didn't think twice about going behind the administration's back. Unfortunately, even though Westport did his best to remedy the situation by sticking to his testimonial and saying how Gilbert had affected his life for the good, Broadstreet hammered away at Gilbert's failure to defend himself, encouraging a heavy silence after Westport was finally dismissed.

Broadstreet had managed to definitely turn the tables on a promising start, and during the break, his smug grin bore testament to that.

Things will all go downhill from here if Gilbert doesn't speak up, Ian thought. When he risked a glance at Rachel, he found her distraught, biting her lip and shaking her head.

He itched to sit next to her, to offer words of comfort or…

Who was he kidding? That wasn't his job.

Ian got back into reporter mode—where he damn well belonged—when Broadstreet reconvened the proceedings and called Kathryn Price to the table for Gilbert.

It was as if the entire hall scooted to the edges of their chairs, waiting to glimpse the statuesque golden girl who'd suffered such pain and tragedy. Murmurs provided a processional for the scarred ex-model as she lifted her chin and made her way to the hot seat. Once there, she smiled at Nate Williams, who returned the affection.

Unable to stop himself, Ian slid another gaze to Rachel, hearing Broadstreet speaking the usual opening greeting to Kathryn.

But then things took a turn.

"You're another character witness who plans to save Gilbert's career?" Broadstreet made it sound like an accusation, as if she would fail to help Gilbert as spectacularly as David Westport had done.

Because the professor wasn't exactly helping himself.

"Yes," she said. "And I've got plenty to say. I hope you're comfortable in that seat."

That brought a chuckle from the audience, and Broadstreet shot them the stink eye. If they were laughing at the slightest excuse from Kathryn, they were doing it to offer aid to Gilbert.

Ian kind of dug that.

Automatically, he noted that Rachel had even perked up. It sent a tiny thrill through him, reawakening the nerve endings on his skin, his sharp awareness of her.

Before Broadstreet could regroup, Kathryn was off and running. Tucking a strand of glossy brown hair behind her ear, she said, "Really, I'm surprised at the board, calling Gilbert out like this. He's helped a lot of students during those *awful, horrifying* office hours that he holds. You know—where the kids gather and generally find some acceptance and understanding. He's not the leader of a cult or staging evil activities under the administration's nose—not like you'd love to think, President Broadstreet. He's changed lives, and to fire a man who can bring out the best in people and help them to see their potential…"

Broadstreet tried to interject, but Kathryn merely held up a finger to quiet him, continuing.

"As a rule, I don't talk about this, but during one of those office hours, Professor Harrison listened to me as I told him about a sexual assault. My *own* assault. So I know the wonders Professor Harrison can work."

The oxygen seemed to leave the room. It certainly left Ian.

"I'm sorry to hear about your troubles, Ms. Price." Broadstreet did look genuinely sorry, though Ian wondered if it was because his momentum had been destroyed.

But Ian decided to give him the benefit of the doubt.

And he could afford to because, suddenly, as Kathryn emotionally related how Gilbert had counseled her out of depression, Ian started to see the light.

Maybe the professor really was a damned hero, just like Rachel had always said. Persecuted by the system, the victim of a misguided man's power trip.

He was someone Ian could relate to, being a true believer in bucking authority himself.

His heart rate picked up speed.

God, what if…

Yeah.

These were times for heroes to emerge, Ian thought, blood pounding in his ears. *Forget the dirt, the drama, the damage.*

What if he could uncover what was *really* going on, show the country that, somewhere on earth, there were still good people? Mentors who came to the rescue. Protégés who would stand up for someone they loved and believed in. Patchwork families who came together in hard times to fight for what was right.

In an age that could use a hero or two, Ian had stumbled upon one at the most unexpected time.

Wouldn't it be great if someone could show this reunion to the rest of the people out there who needed some real news and positive truth?

Someone like…

Energized, Ian watched Gilbert Harrison shine a look of astonishing affection on Kathryn, who smiled back at him with adoration.

Someone like Ian himself. Someone who would uncover what was really going on and report the truth.

It was a headline that might not sell a lot of papers, but one that could—maybe—save his own soul.

If it wasn't already too far gone.

Chapter Three

That night, Rachel took a shower, then slipped into some cozy flannel pajamas to eat a popcorn dinner and watch TV. Her friends had indeed met at the tavern after the hearing, but a phone call from Jane had informed Rachel that the gang still disagreed about telling Gilbert that they knew about him being the benefactor.

Why upset their mentor right now? they'd decided yet again. Gilbert didn't need to know that they were all aware of his secret, especially since Ella Gardner, the only person who was supposed to know, could talk him into going public herself.

Besides, if they all kept their mouths shut, Ian Beck would have less of a chance of discovering Gilbert's business. After all, the professor had kept his benefactor status under wraps for years. No one knew why, precisely, but he'd obviously been intent on maintaining his privacy.

More remorseful than ever about avoiding another gang meeting *and* going behind their backs with Ian, Rachel sat down on her couch, popcorn bowl on her lap, and found her favorite old Hitchcock movie on cable. She was trying to escape again, but it wasn't any use.

The next time my friends ask for my company, she thought, *I need to go. I miss them.*

As if in answer to her musings, a knock sounded at her door.

She tiptoed over the worn carpet, coming to peek out of the lace curtains by the door. *Oh, no.*

Bathed by the porch light, Ian Beck saw her spying on him, a smile lighting over his lips as he raised his hand in a friendly wave.

Rachel darted away from the window, thrown off guard. "What in the world…?"

She glanced down at her faded yellow pajamas, the flannel design featuring waddling ducks. Yeesh, there were even dialogue balloons with the word "Quack!" in them.

Her first instinct was to run to her room for a robe, but the darn thing was so raggedy that it made her pajamas look like J-Lo's newest Academy Awards ensemble in comparison.

Ian knocked again. "You still there?" he asked through the door.

"Yes." She paused. "I'm not really dressed for company."

"Oh, the duck pajamas. I saw them when you just looked through the window. They're cute."

So much for fooling old X-ray eyes. But why did it matter? Was she really out to impress this guy?

An unbidden blush answered that for her.

In response, Rachel unlocked her door, determined to prove herself wrong. Maybe duck pajamas would kill the tension or...whatever it was between them. Flannel wasn't exactly the new lingerie.

She opened the door a crack, letting in a stream of chilled air. Ian was breathing plumes of smoke, his hands stuffed into his jacket pockets, his face reddened by the weather.

"Don't tell me," she said. "You want another interview."

"Not...exactly." He shuffled around, doing a subtle cold dance.

She was going to have to invite him in, wasn't she?

Opening the door the rest of the way, she ushered him over the threshold, anxiously tugging at the bottom of her pajama top as if that would turn it into a fashionable sweater.

"Damn, it feels good in here, and it smells like popcorn," he said, peering around her modest home, absolutely unaware that she was considering putting it on the market by the end of the month.

Or maybe, she thought, *I could get a full-time job, a second job or... Or what? Debtor's prison?*

After closing the door, she gestured toward the bowl of popcorn on the couch. "I'm settled in for the night."

"That's what you do on a Friday?" He shrugged out of his jacket and allowed her to drape it over a dining chair. "You're a homebody."

She'd developed the habit with Isaac. On Fridays after work, he would stop by the video store and rent kung fu videos, buying one per month to add to his collection. Sonny Chiba, Bruce Lee, Jackie Chan—she was well acquainted with the boys, but watching those kinds of flicks didn't appeal to her anymore. They'd only been fun with her husband around.

Still, the homebody habit remained, especially nowadays, when she could make herself feel better just by hanging out alone. So much for being the belle of the social scene anymore.

"I outgrew the weekend bar thing a long time ago," she said. "I'd rather hole in and get to bed early."

The mention of a bed seemed to stop the flow of air around them. Suddenly, the TV's volume seemed way too loud, her pajamas much too revealing, her bare feet too vulnerable.

Even standing a few feet away from him felt too close, as if his skin was giving off more heat than she could handle.

"Can I get you something to drink?" She took off toward the sofa and grabbed the popcorn, then veered toward the kitchen, trying to put some distance between their bodies.

Ian followed her with his gaze, a lopsided grin revealing that he knew how nervous she was.

"I'll have whatever you're having," he said.

After setting the bowl on the counter, she got two bottled waters out of the refrigerator. It was the most harmless beverage she could think of. "So what brings you around? The hearing wasn't enough for you today?"

"I don't blame you for being frustrated. It couldn't have been easy, sitting there and listening to Broadstreet manipulate whatever Westport or Kathryn had to say." Ian sauntered over to the counter, where he half sat on a barstool that showed a tiny tear on one side. "Just when things were starting to look good, he turned it around. And I don't think Gilbert was helping by just sitting there and taking Broadstreet's knocks."

"We all thought Kathryn's testimony was going well until Broadstreet started second-guessing Gilbert's good intentions."

Rachel urged the bowl of popcorn at him, then uncapped both waters. She took a swig of hers, as if quelling her temper.

Damn Alex Broadstreet. After Kathryn had shed such wonderful light on Gilbert's caring nature, Broadstreet had tried to make it seem as if the professor had shirked his duty by failing to get his student proper guidance from a "real" mental-care professional. In essence, Gilbert had come off as inept and arrogant.

And, as Ian had pointed out, Gilbert hadn't even lifted a finger in his own defense. He was guarding his secrets carefully. But why?

As she lowered the bottle, she realized that Ian had been carefully gauging her. Her blood gave a shuddering thump, leaving her heart racing.

"Monday's another day," Ian said. "Nate Williams and Jacob Weber are bound to present strong testimony. They'll give Broadstreet a run for his money."

She didn't want to think about next week, because she would be testifying, too. Boy, how would *she* stand up to the board president? He was going to tear her apart.

Ian must have picked up on her fear, because he reached out, placed his hand over the one she was resting on the counter. The contact sheltered her in warm calm, spiking her skin with tingles.

"You're surrounded by friends," he said. "I couldn't help but notice how supportive you are of one another. In fact, afterward, I saw Ella Gardner giving Gilbert a pep talk."

For a sublime moment, she was almost able to block out reality, to concentrate on his palm covering the back of her hand.

But she had also seen Ella and Gilbert, and the memory intruded upon any comfort she might have felt from Ian's touch. Ella, who'd been ahead of Rachel in school by several years, had been very close to the professor, too. When Rachel had seen her talking to him after the hearing, she'd been struck by her friend's pleading gestures, the desperation written on her face. Rachel knew that the pregnant woman had been trying to convince Gilbert to confess that he was the benefactor, but of course, the older man had sat there shaking his head, apparently resolute and clueless to the fact that the rest of the gang was already armed with the truth.

Why can't he just admit it? Rachel wondered once again. Can't he see the revelation would only help his cause?

She felt Ian's hand tighten over hers. Instinctively, she turned her palm upward. His skin was rough, masculine, strong in its reassurance. When he rubbed his thumb near hers, the easy caress took her breath away.

But then she glanced into his eyes—those intense reporter's weapons. All the questions he was harboring speared into her and, suddenly, she remembered who they both were.

A journalist.

And his prey.

She backed away from him, disconnecting, crossing her arms over her chest. "Why are you here again?"

On the counter, his hand closed, just like the mouth of a predator after it realizes that its last meal has escaped.

But Ian's posture told a different story. For a moment, he seemed sad, lost in an entirely different way.

"I just…" He straightened in his chair, shrugged. "I wanted you to know what I saw today, what I'm going to report—a man being railroaded."

Excellent! But…he could've phoned her with this news.

Was it possible that he only wanted to see her again, and that's why he'd shown up on her doorstep?

Before Rachel could get too excited, she dissuaded herself from believing it.

Instead, she looked askance at him. "I thought you were supposed to sit on the fence, to stand back and report the facts."

"Yeah. That's how it's supposed to be. But sometimes it's impossible to divorce yourself from a story, especially when there's real injustice. The more I learn about Gilbert Harrison, the more I suspect Alex Broadstreet's motives."

Her arms slipped from their protective position across her chest as he continued.

"I'm more surprised at my feelings than anyone," he said, laughing a little, "but I was getting riled at that hearing. I've even had this pinch of…I don't know what it is…anger?…that Gilbert is going to come out on the wrong side of everything and—you know what? That's wrong. A Good Samaritan is taking a beating from an authority figure and I can't stop it."

Rachel refused to comment. Had Ian found proof that Gilbert was the benefactor? No. He couldn't. He would've come right out and said it by now. He was only talking in generalities.

"It doesn't sit right with me," he added. "Hell, but what do I know? Gilbert won't agree to an interview, so I have no basis for a personal opinion."

Rachel's heart crashed to the tile. "Ah. So that's it. You want me to set up an interview with him."

Of course. That was the reason for Ian's home invasion. He wanted to work his wiles on her in person, probably knowing she was a sucker where Gilbert's well-being was concerned.

Ian ran a finger over the rim of the popcorn bowl, his brow furrowed. "Even though I'd like nothing better than to talk with him, that's not why I'm here, Rachel. I…" He shook his head. "Damn, I'm not sure why I came."

She chanced a look at him, finding that he was doing the same. When their gazes locked, her pulse paused…stretched…*popped,* forcing her to glance away.

The room seemed entirely too small with him in it. Alarmingly, space only seemed to shrink more and more with every tick of the clock on the fireplace mantel.

But the last thing she wanted to do was acknowledge the taunt awareness, the sensual snap in the air.

This couldn't be happening. Couldn't he see the barriers between them…his job, the color of her skin?

"Who would've thunk it?" she said, evading the moment. "You're actually a crusader, Ian Beck."

"Not me." He sighed, grinned, grabbed some popcorn and rattled it around in his closed hand. The cavalier journalist had returned, thank goodness. "I haven't been a pen-wielding warrior for a while. But if Gilbert manages to get his fat pulled out of the fire, I wouldn't mind seeing it."

As he tossed the food into his mouth, he seemed much too casual. Was he lying to her? Did Ian Beck really have a softer side? Not that he'd admit to it.

Still, this new possibility prodded her to talk—really talk—about what was happening. More than anything, she wanted to spill her doubts and fears about Gilbert, to lean on someone else's shoulder in order to take the burden off of her own.

Be careful, she told herself. This man is an investigative reporter. Don't you think he's used this act before? Don't you think this is how he gets his dirt?

Even so, the thought of revealing everything to a person who wouldn't be around for much longer was tempting. After he was gone, her confessions would leave town with him, too, as if she'd never spoken at all.

A stranger, she thought. *A temporary haven.*

Then reality slapped her upside the head. The last person she wanted to blab to was a journalist, for heaven's sake. But if he were any other friendly companion, she knew she'd really give some serious thought to allowing a man like Ian Beck to give her some relief.

And maybe even in more ways than one.

Fleetingly, she imagined leaning her head against his chest, closing her eyes as he enveloped her with his strong arms, breathing easy as he stroked her back, his hands slipping under her shirt to caress her bare skin.

Warmed by the fantasy, she smiled at him, then tentatively walked closer, reaching in to the bowl for a handful of popcorn.

Unexpectedly, he did the same thing.

Their fingers brushed, sending giddy shivers up her arm, through her skin, down to her belly.

"If you want," he said softly, keeping his hand near hers, "I can show you my rough draft tomorrow. You can give me your thumbs-up before my deadline."

Wow, he was really trying to earn her trust and reel her in.

Curiously, she skimmed her finger over his as she picked up a kernel, acting as if the contact was an accident, even if they both knew it wasn't. As she brought the food to her mouth, he didn't look at the popcorn so much as her lips.

She allowed herself to rest the snack against her mouth, enjoying his frank interest, still thrown off balance by it, too. "Thank you. I'd really like that."

Pushing the snack into her mouth, she knew what he was probably thinking: that she wasn't merely liking the chance to preview his reporting.

That there were so many other things for her to like about him.

Things that just might get her through these troubled times.

After polishing off the popcorn last night, Ian had offered to take Rachel out for a more substantial dinner, but she had declined, saying that she planned to get up early for a painting class at the local learning center.

Even though he knew there was a current of attraction running between them like a live wire, he'd accepted her excuse, thanked her for the snack and made arrangements to meet her at the art shop the next morning.

Back in his hotel room, he'd burned the midnight oil, punching out his story on his laptop, satisfied enough with the results to get a few hours of shut-eye.

Morning didn't come soon enough. But when it did, he shined himself up, sent an e-mail to a loop he'd created for his nine nieces and nephews and, by the time eleven o'clock rolled around, traveled by subway to meet Rachel.

Her class was located in a shop on a quiet, tree-lined block that included knitting and crocheting boutiques, a small Italian restaurant and an antique emporium. Thank God the place was tiny enough so that he could see the students through the lettering of the front window. Ian didn't go into these kinds of stores unless he was chasing a story. And it'd have to be a damned good one, at that.

Rachel was sitting near the front, painting a plaster-cast bust. It resembled an old sailor, with a burnished yellow hat, slicker-coated shoulders and overgrown whiskers covering his craggy face.

Paintbrush held in the air as she tilted her head and considered her nearly finished masterpiece, Rachel frowned. She set down the tool and pushed herself away from the table, as if she was done with the project, abandoning it.

Ian lightly rapped on the window, catching her attention.

When she saw him, a smile beamed over her face. Unadulterated joy traveled to her eyes, absolutely transforming her.

Shocking him.

He actually had to blink, to clear his gaze.

But... Yup, there she was, still smiling, and now waving.

Somehow, Ian had made her happy just by showing up. He'd never seen such a reaction, not from a woman, anyway. Sure, his family tended to jump all over him like white on rice whenever he could come to one of their shindigs in Albany, but this was different.

This was...

...scary.

And real nice.

He waved back, and she set about cleaning up. Soon she was saying goodbye to the teacher and exiting the shop while donning her long coat.

A blush covered her skin, giving a hint of rose to the creamy brown of her cheeks. It was almost as if she'd noted her strong reaction at seeing him earlier and was doing her damnedest to make him think he'd been imagining her excitement.

"Good work," he said as they began to walk. "Your sailor looked like he just walked off a ship."

"You think so?" She frowned. "The colors were all wrong. I don't know… I have no talent for painting anything. Not even plaster."

He didn't like how she was doubting herself. "Hey you've got some art magic going. Your work was great."

"Not really. There's not much point in taking more classes if all I'm doing is creating visual barf." She laughed. "That won't make the world a more beautiful place at all."

"Don't be so hard on yourself." Impulsively, he stopped, rested his hands on her shoulders. "I'm not blowing sunshine in your ear. It was really good."

Her eyes had gone wide. Was it because of the compliment or because he was touching her again? Jeez, he couldn't seem to keep his hands to himself around her.

"You're fooling me," she said in a soft voice.

"No fooling here."

A beat passed, one with a hint of all the words they weren't saying—not that Ian could even identify what those words would be even if he had the guts to blurt them out.

As Rachel offered a shy grin, then started to walk away, Ian stood there a moment, hands empty, wondering what the hell was going on. Wondering why she didn't fit into his seamless no-attachments-no-worries life like every other woman did.

Within four steps, he caught up to her.

"I'm sorry about that," she said.

"What?"

"Being so whiny. Grubbing for compliments."

He hadn't thought it was a big deal, but now he wasn't so sure her self-critique had been that simple.

Women, he thought. Each of them a puzzle. Impossible to understand.

So why did he *want* to solve her so badly?

"I'm the type of person," she said, "who constantly flits from one activity to the next, one club to the other. Gilbert always told me that I seek approval from outside sources, and I leave before I don't get it. And he's right. Back in school, I was Miss Popularity. I was the head of everything from Pep Club to Drama Club to the Cheer Squad—'the star.'" She smiled. "But those were the days when I had the energy to do it all, when I fueled myself with social activities and loved the attention."

She followed up with a small, sad laugh, and Ian filed that away. It was confirmation of everything he'd feared about her: a lover who would require much more care than he normally invested.

Someone he'd have to change for.

But…

Damn, he couldn't believe he was even thinking about it.

His family and friends had always teased him that someday he'd find a woman worth the commitment and effort.

Was Rachel James that woman?

"Were you ever a joiner?" she asked, oblivious to his world veering off its course.

"Me?" He forced himself back into bachelor mode. Much easier that way. "I can't say I've joined a whole lot. But once I do, I'm loyal. I've had this reporting gig since I was twenty-nine, seven years now, and the adrenaline was what always kept me going. I could always count on it to get me from one day to the next."

Interesting, how that had all come out in the past tense.

"So, tell me…" Without warning, she stopped walking, looking around as if confused. "Hey, you know what? Where are we going?"

Good question. It just occurred to him that they'd started talking the second she'd come out the door, ignoring the details around them, so happy to see each other that they hadn't even decided where they were headed.

"Isn't there a coffee house around?" he asked. "We can go over my article there."

"Two blocks away." She tugged at his jacket and started down the sidewalk again. "So, as I was asking, you're pretty good at sticking with one thing?"

Jobs, yes, he thought. *But not with much else.*

"My career allows me a lot of freedom, so I'm not too stifled." Or, at least, it *had* offered freedom. "I'm content with it." Or, at least, he *had* been.

"Running around from assignment to assignment must make it tough to put down roots."

"It *is* hard to settle down. And I feel for any woman who decides to hook up with a reporter. My last assignment was over in Saudi Arabia—not exactly someplace, at the moment, to encourage thoughts of safe harbor for a boyfriend."

She was watching him in a new way—not like he was a muckraker or a tragedy chaser. He puffed up a little, flattered and kind of proud.

"How did you go from a hot spot to Saunders?" she asked.

"Well, even an action junkie like me needs a break every once in a while. I thought I could do this story in my sleep. I have to write one of those every once in a while to stay sane, you know."

Too bad he hadn't known what kind of complete sleaze had been on his editor's agenda. The second Ian got back to the offices in New York, he was going to put in for another overseas assignment, just to wash away the bad taste of this one.

They were passing a toy boutique, and Ian slowed, checking out the window display. He pointed to a compact bunny wearing a Red Sox uniform.

"Mind if we stop?" he asked.

"You're into furry little stuffed things?" She laughed. "Wow, Ian, you manage to surprise me at least once a day."

Just think what I could do if I had more time, he thought.

"It'll take one second and that's it," he said, heading for the store's entrance.

Five minutes later, he had the bag-wrapped bunny in his jacket pocket.

"For the brood back home," he said. "My nephews and nieces. All nine of them."

"Whoa, one bunny for the masses?"

He grinned, just thinking of the kids. Just thinking of how his parents and four brothers good-naturedly ribbed him for being the one sibling who wasn't contributing to Beck World Domination by breeding too much. He always had a good comeback for that, saying that he wasn't one to add to overpopulation. They should *thank* him.

"We have this game," Ian said as they came to a corner and paused. The coffee house was across the busy street. "Every time I go on assignment, I get some kind of item that represents the area: a toy, a trinket, a symbol. I pose it in an interesting place and take a picture, as if it's visiting right along with me. Then I send it over an e-mail loop to my little nieces and nephews—a postcard. When I get home, I hide it, and one lucky boy or girl becomes the proud new owner when they find it. I started this when my brothers told me that I was bringing the kids too many souvenirs and they were getting spoiled. But I still give them each something tiny from all my travels, even if it's candy. That's a big secret, though."

"I won't tell."

She seemed about near to bursting with approval. He couldn't help reaching for her hand, enfolding it in his own. Warmth shot through his fingers.

"Time to cross the street," he said, ignoring the flare of sweet hunger, the compulsion to gather her into his arms and hold her close.

When the traffic allowed, they sprinted to the coffee shop and took a table by the window. He held on to her hand the entire way.

And she didn't let go, either, until they were inside and ready to order at the counter.

Unfortunately, that's when her cell phone rang. She had to use both hands to unzip her purse, so there went his big moment. His skin felt cold and bereft, having gotten used to the pressure of her fingers entwined with his own.

Answering the call, she indicated that he should go ahead and order while she claimed a table.

Soon afterward, he joined her with two cups of cappuccino. He'd had to guess at what beverage she would enjoy the most and, judging from her enthusiastic nod, he'd done well.

Ian tried not to be too happy about that, but he was. Dammit all, he was.

"Okay," Rachel said, obviously winding up the call. She sucked in a breath, looking as if she was making an important decision, then exhaled on her final answer. "I'll be there."

From the look on her face, Ian guessed she'd just jumped some kind of mental hurdle, one that didn't necessarily comfort her.

"That was Jane," she said, folding up her phone and putting it away. "Breakfast tomorrow with the gang."

Ah, he thought. *She's finally hanging out with her friends again outside of the trial. But why?* "Is the team forming battle plans?"

"Yeah. I suppose it's about time I was a part of the group again."

Cello music from the speakers played over their silence as they drank. The change in tone rattled him, made him crazy to get back the past fifteen minutes.

What could he... Hey, talking about his family had entertained her. Maybe asking about *hers* would do the same trick.

"How about the James clan?" he ventured. "How many nieces and nephews overrun all your reunions?"

She gulped down her cappuccino, tightening her hold on the porcelain mug almost imperceptibly. But after a pause, she answered, "My sister's too young to be a mom...fourteen. And, actually, she's not even my real sister."

"Oh." Had he stumbled upon the wrong subject? Judging by the darkness haunting her gaze, he guessed so.

Was it too late to backpedal?

She forced a smile. "I'm adopted, if that's what you're wondering."

Something told him to shut up, to can the reporter sense and leave well enough alone.

Luckily, she saved his bacon, rescuing him from making a further nuisance of himself because—God knows—that's the last thing he wanted to be for this woman.

"So where's that rough draft?" she asked, her perky tone ringing false.

Relieved, he couldn't get the papers out from the lining of his jacket soon enough. "For your pleasure."

At that, she really did smile, small dimples forming at the tips of her mouth. The gesture bowled Ian over, making him wonder if he'd be no more than a fallen pin by the end of the assignment he'd come to despise.

An assignment he was actually enjoying more than he would like to.

Chapter Four

The next morning, someone unexpected was waiting for Rachel at the restaurant.

Someone Professor Gilbert Harrison knew Rachel had been avoiding for a while now.

Him.

As Gilbert sat on pins and needles, a fire crackled in the hearth near his table, lending the dark-wooded room a warm glow. The air was permeated by the aroma of syrup and butter, making his stomach fist.

But maybe those were only nerves tumbling through him, anxiety at seeing his favorite student again. Fear at having Rachel look into him with that troubled gaze of hers.

His hands trembled as he held the menu, as he anticipated her reaction at seeing that her friends hadn't come to breakfast and had merely set the two of them up to dine together in solitude.

Steady, Gilbert, he thought. *You've gotten this far without life crumbling down around you. Don't give up hope now.*

Minutes later, when the restaurant hostess led Rachel into the room, relief poured through him and he couldn't help smiling. But then, as his ex-student took in the scene and realized that Jane had lured her into a trap by lying about a group breakfast, his anxiety built up again.

"Good morning," he said, getting to his feet and maintaining the grin. He couldn't help it—smiling was so natural around her.

And such a chore nowadays.

"Gilbert."

Her dark eyes glittered with what he thought might be a mixture of happiness and sadness. He had never intended to visit pain upon her, had never wanted anything but the best for her and all of his other students.

Things just hadn't turned out as he had planned.

After he held out her chair, she sat down, then aimed her own hesitant smile at him.

There.

It was as if she had opened up a cloudy sky to show him sunshine. Contentment flooded him, and he expelled the breath he had been holding.

While he sat, Rachel took off her coat. "I'm guessing that Jane and the others won't be eating with us."

"You would guess correctly."

She nodded and inspected her menu, slightly discomfited.

"Is that okay?" he asked. "Us being alone."

"Sure." She peered up at him, laughed. "Of course. Of course it's okay. I'm sure they wanted me to spend some time with you since we've both been so busy lately. I'm more than glad about it, too, even if Jane felt they had to be sneaky."

At least she was perceptive enough to realize that everyone thought something was wrong with her. The gang had plotted to get Rachel alone with Gilbert because they thought he would be the one who could dig around and find out why she had been so oddly quiet, why she had suddenly been refusing invitations to socialize and interact with them. After all, he had been so much like a parent to her over the years—seeing as her own mother and father were so ambivalent—that it was normal for him to offer guidance. And even if Rachel had been just as standoffish with him recently, he was still the best candidate to help her.

He was the man everyone could depend on.

Or, rather, that was how it used to be. The hearing had strained his prized relationships because all his secrets were crawling out of their hiding places, challenging everyone's trust in him, threatening to ruin all the good deeds he had promised to keep silent so long ago.

And some deeds he wished he could make up for.

He chanced a gaze at Rachel, who had gone back to selecting her food.

His favorite, he thought. His greatest failure.

"I know the timing stinks with the hearing and all," she said, closing the menu, "but I've been so busy that I can barely keep my head on straight. You know how it is, how badly I handle pressure. But I wanted to have breakfast with the group this morning, to be involved with brainstorming ideas for your so-called rescue."

Excuses. She was hiding something much more painful. He knew Rachel too well for her to misdirect him. Still, it was a good sign that she had wanted to show up for Jane's invitation. It signaled that maybe Rachel was ready to open up a little.

"Everyone only wants to see you more," he said. "It's not like you to be the reticent one."

"I'll be back to normal as soon as I go through all my finances and decide if I need to sell the house. I'm going nuts with my head full of numbers right now."

Gilbert leaned forward. "You know I can lend you money."

She tucked a curly strand of dark hair away from her face, clearly embarrassed. "That's the last thing you need to be doing, Gilbert. What if—worst-case scenario—you get fired?"

"I've saved up a nest egg. Don't worry."

Nest egg. For Pete's sake, he wished he could tell her about the inheritance he had received from his grand-father—the money he had been using to give anonymous gifts to those who needed it the most over the years.

The money he had privately sworn to keep secret from the rest of his family, so as not to cause a feud. Grandfather Harrison had known that Gilbert would not squander the inheritance, had known that he would use the funds wisely and carry on with his tradition of aiding others. Unfortunately, the favoritism had come with a stipulation that hadn't been mentioned in the will: secrecy.

Something Gilbert had gotten in the habit of relying on.

Something Gilbert was paying for to this day, even though hiding the truth had kept the family together, just as Gilbert had known it would.

After the waitress took their orders, Rachel said, "I wish I were as calm about everything as you are."

In spite of the encouraging statement, Gilbert knew what she had to be thinking: that he was certainly collected—too much so. That he had aged twenty years during these past few months, the price he paid for internalizing the horror of what was happening to him at Saunders.

He didn't want to worry her by admitting that, deep inside, he was a mess, terrified that he would lose the job he lived for and lose all the students who were like the children he and his wife hadn't been able to create.

"How are things at home?" she asked.

He smiled, so thankful to have her back. There was

still a bit of distance between them, but she cared. That was all that mattered.

"Things at home are…quiet," he said. "With Mary gone, the sofa doesn't seem as comfortable. Dinner alone at the table doesn't taste as good. You know what I mean."

Sympathetically, Rachel leaned her elbows on the table and tilted her head. She was a widow just as much as he was a widower, only Gilbert had lost Mary eight months ago. Sometimes it felt like mere days.

"There are times," he said, "when I feel like she's in the next room, just sleeping. Or that you're with her, feeding her, taking care of her."

"I miss Mary, too."

"I know. She adored you. During her last days, it meant the world for you to be there with us."

"Thank you. You know, if you ever need to vent, I can relate…"

"I'm fine." Basically. But he still didn't like to be reminded of Mary's death or of Isaac. That man—as kind as he'd been, Gilbert grudgingly admitted—had persuaded Rachel to desert the dreams Gilbert had been helping her to build. He had taken her away from a solid education that could have aimed her life in glorious directions—an education Gilbert had made possible for Rachel by arranging financial aid on the sly.

She still didn't know that, but it was only one of a hundred things he was keeping to himself.

Swamped by remorse, Gilbert didn't have enough appetite to even consider eating when the food arrived.

Instead, he managed to look occupied by moving the eggs and hash browns around with his fork. Rachel was echoing his movements, taking her time in spreading cream cheese on her bagel.

"Rachel, why don't you have some of my food? You aren't eating enough to fill a bird."

"No, this is good." She bit into her meal with zest, as if to prove him wrong.

As she chewed, she tugged at her shapeless, oversize sweater, then averted her gaze.

Rachel had always been sensitive about her figure, her half-and-half skin. She had always tried to overcompensate for her status as a "social outcast" by being the star of the campus and joining enough clubs so that her grades ended up suffering.

Lord forgive him, Gilbert wanted to talk some sense into the people who had raised her. They had branded her with a debilitating inferiority complex. From countless office hours, he had learned about how her adoptive parents had casually teased her about "trading our light-skinned daughter in for a darker model like us" or not being "one of them." When Rachel was fifteen, they had gone on to have their own miracle baby. According to Rachel, the child looked just like her mother and father, and they prized little Jeanne high above their first daughter. This had scarred Rachel for life, even if that hadn't been the intention. Gilbert couldn't stop wondering how she would have turned out if he had been there for her earlier.

By now, Rachel had stopped eating to watch him, her brow knitted as if she wanted to say something yet didn't have the wherewithal. He had seen this face so many times before, had done everything in his power to make the anguish go away.

A power he wasn't sure he had anymore.

"Gilbert…"

Her words choked off. His pulse seemed to stop, too, addled by fear.

She knew something, didn't she? But what? Which one of his secrets had she uncovered? Had Ella told her that he was the campus's secret benefactor?

Or had Cassidy told her…?

No. She would never betray Gilbert, not with something that could be so hurtful to Rachel. He had done too good a job of hiding that particular truth over the years, keeping it locked inside a safe—and himself—while it attempted to gnaw its way out of his chest.

But at the same time, he wished Rachel *did* know.

While he waited, everything moved in slow motion around them.

But just as she seemed to be on the edge of saying her piece, she closed her mouth, shut her eyes, shook her head. Guilt resumed its destructive path through his bloodstream.

Gilbert didn't even want to ask what she had been about to say. He couldn't.

No, instead he changed the subject altogether, to something safer.

"Nate says you're impressing everyone in your new job with your paralegal skills, Rachel."

She paused, unable to fight a smile. He had made her proud. It was something he had always been able to do in order to bolster the confidence of his favorite student.

"I'm really enjoying the work," she said. "I'm glad you and Nate set me up with the job. It's part-time right now, but I'm hoping to work my way into more hours."

"Well, from what I hear, you'll do it. Strong help is tough to come by."

"Nate's been a saint." Rachel left three-quarters of her bagel untouched on the plate. "He's even coaching me for my testimonial this week."

"Now, don't worry about that. I only asked you to speak on my behalf because…"

Because I'm desperate to keep my job, he thought.

"I know. You want to showcase the people you've helped the most. And, Gilbert, when I go up there, I'm going to make Alex Broadstreet's head spin."

That's my girl, Gilbert thought.

"And," she added, "I think public sentiment will be on your side."

Here, she flushed, spiking Gilbert's interest. She looked as if she had her own secret, a wish tucked within her heart.

He wondered if this prediction about public reaction had anything to do with the reporter who had been skulking around campus—and Rachel.

Ian Beck. That was the man's name.

Before he could start asking questions, Rachel sighed, wearing a beatific smile that quieted Gilbert. He hadn't seen her glow like this for years, and he wasn't about to shatter whatever was going on inside of her.

No, instead, the professor dug into his breakfast, satisfied for now to be sitting across from her again, just like he had during office hours, when she would seek him out for advice, for the assurance she truly needed.

Because, if she *did* find out everything he had been secreting, she might not ever want to see Gilbert again.

Monday morning welcomed a gray sky, but that didn't keep Rachel from humming as she ambled down the sidewalk to the subway stop.

She was going to be optimistic about today's portion of the hearing. And why not? Life was good.

Although yesterday's breakfast with Gilbert hadn't exactly been filled with hurrahs and lighthearted moments, it had been a relief to realize that she could eventually work up the courage to share confidences with him again. And she'd come so close, a heartbeat away from asking him about the adoption papers, but she'd chickened out.

Still, she'd taken the first step toward broaching the subject. That was a positive sign, right? And the reminder of Gilbert's soothing nature made her think the both of them would eventually come clean with each other and repair their relationship enough to start over.

If she could take another baby step and actually pose the question next time.

Gilbert, why are you in possession of such personal papers? And who exactly is Rosemary Johnson?

Rachel pictured the name again, imagined a woman who was so much a part of her life, but not really a part at all.

Rosemary, she thought, *I'd give anything to meet you. I've wanted to know you my whole life, dreamed about you, made up stories about you.*

Why did you give me up?

Deep in concentration, Rachel almost didn't notice the newspaper stand when she walked by it.

Wait, she thought. *Ian's story. It's been published!*

She backtracked and bought a copy from a friendly vendor with a gold tooth and a crinkly-eyed smile. Eagerly, she scanned for the article and found it near the bottom of the front page.

Hah, Alex Broadstreet, she thought, *you're not going to recover from this blow.*

But then she absorbed the caption. *Scheming Professor Accused of Inappropriate Conduct with Students:* Administrator asks community to censure unscrupulous faculty member.

Rachel hesitated, then checked the banner to see that she was indeed reading the *National Sun*.

But this couldn't be… Oh. Of course. This was probably about *another* hearing.

She skimmed the article to see if she was right.

Blah, blah…Saunders University…Professor Gilbert Harrison…President Alex Broadstreet…

Oh, God.

Her throat tightening with oncoming tears, she finally sought the byline, dreading what she knew would already be there.

"By Ian Beck," she whispered.

As she stood on the sidewalk, too stunned to move, passersby streamed around her, bumping her in their haste to get to work.

He'd played her for an ever-loving fool, hadn't he? Jerk. And…idiot. Damn, she was an *idiot*.

Lowering her head, she tried to block out their time together this past weekend. Friday night popcorn. Saturday morning coffee.

For heaven's sake, she'd even started to get personal with him, listening with keen interest as he talked about his family, hinting to him about the hard times in her own.

Thank goodness she hadn't followed her heart and allowed him past the threshold of it. Thank goodness she hadn't told him much of anything about Gilbert…

…yet.

Because, truth to tell, she'd been close to doing it. Oh, yeah, she'd started feeling cozy with Ian Beck, trusting him as a person and forgetting he was a lowdown, cement-sucking, money-hungry reporter.

An emphatic nudge from a random shoulder caused Rachel to stumble. Gradually, she focused on the people around her, customers who might have already read about their local university. Gullible folks who might already believe the worst about a professor who didn't deserve to be hung out to dry.

And how do you know that, Rachel?

It was a voice in the back of her mind, a tone that sang of lullabies and big, warm meals cooked in a steaming kitchen.

A voice that Rosemary Johnson, her real mother, might have had.

Yes, how *did* Rachel know that Gilbert was innocent?

But, more immediately, how had Ian Beck's promise turned into a nasty indictment against the professor?

Gathering her strength and temper, Rachel tucked the paper under her arm and headed for the subway.

Because she was sure as fire going to find out.

Crap, Ian thought as he slapped the morning edition of the *National Sun* against his thigh.

And "crap" was the politest of all the words he was thinking.

He and Joe were sitting on a bench near Lumley Hall, awaiting the main players in the big production of Gilbert's Hearing, Act Two. But now, after having read his article, he wasn't so much looking forward to seeing Rachel again.

Even if he'd spent all of yesterday daydreaming about her, itching to invent an excuse to call her and invite her out.

"That weenie micromanager chopped the story into

bits and rewrote it," Ian said. "When Edgar asked for my notes, I told him he'd better not slice and dice."

Joe leaned back and rested a hand on his ample belly. His camera hung around his neck, ready for action. "Edgar the Eeee-vil Editor. That's what they're calling him in the lunchroom."

"I've got better names for him." Ian chucked the paper toward the nearest wastebasket. "So much for seven years of establishing a reputation as a reporter people can trust. You know what I'm going to do? I'm going to go over Edgar's head with this, call the boss and get some editor ass fired."

And he knew it would work, too. Ian was a personal favorite of multimillionaire Copley Willens, the owner and publisher. The older man had always told Ian that he was on track for a Pulitzer, so he was sure he'd have the big boss's ear.

"Can I listen in?" Absently, Joe spotted some students arguing near the hall and snapped a picture.

"No, you can get to work. Now, scram while I raise some hell."

With a good-natured shrug, Joe went about his job while Ian got to his feet and dialed New York. Willens's assistant put the call right through to the millionaire, which told Ian something about his standing. After relating his concerns—and he was so very professional about it—Willens said he would call a meeting with Edgar the Editor that morning.

Ian wasn't positive the underling would get fired, but

he'd sure get his tail fried. Hopefully, that would be good enough.

And if it wasn't, there'd be hell to pay.

When Ian finished, he was still stewing, but he needed to get to work right along with Joe, and he did—for about ten minutes.

Because that's when Rachel arrived.

He could tell right away that she was fit to be tied. It was in her stride, the stiff set of her shoulders.

Resigned to being raked over the coals, he waited for her by a bush off to the side of the hall, where they'd be assured a measure of privacy.

When she got within ten feet of him, she held up the paper as if it were the torch of justice—one that had been gutted but was still smoking.

"From the hangdog look on your face," she said, voice feisty, "I think you know what I'm about to say."

"Believe me, I'd like nothing better than to explain."

"Ugh." She dropped the morning edition as if it were a piece of dung. "What ticks me off the most is that I started to put some faith in your nobility, Ian."

Her words were a blade through his chest. Without thinking, he said, "Wait, wait…you *can* do that."

Whoa. Emote a little? When had he gotten so involved that the thought of her disappointment racked his guts?

Her eyes had gone wide, her lips parted as if a come-back had died midway out of her lungs.

"Rachel," he said, voice soft and very much different than the smooth tone he'd normally be using for this sort of fast-talking situation. "Will you just listen to what I have to say?"

"As long as you don't lie to me."

She sounded choked, and that just about killed Ian right there. He wanted her to smile again, to inch a little closer as her confidence in his abilities and honor grew by the day.

He explained about his editor, the phone call to Willens, the hopeful turnaround of the newspaper into something respectable again.

When he finished, she was shaking her head.

"What?" he asked.

"You. Journalism. The assignment. I'm always going to be on guard with you."

"Rachel—"

"Your editor took your notes and bent them to his satisfaction, Ian. Alex Broadstreet does that with words, too. I feel like it's not safe to say anything around either of you."

A dead weight splashed into his belly, and he kept himself from reaching out to pull her to him, to show her she could trust a guy who wasn't sure what the truth was anymore—in this story *and* in life.

But he didn't do it. Breaking down and baring those tenuous urges would dull his edges. Ian was sure of it. Dammit, it was bad enough that he was getting all soft, thinking about everyday heroes and flannel-pajama ducks and anything else that Rachel James had introduced him to.

At a standoff, they watched each other. The crowd shuffled past them, heading for the hall, and he knew that he'd have to get going if he wanted to continue reporting this story.

"Maybe we need to talk afterward," he said, hardly believing his ears because there he went again. Getting soft.

Where was his edge?

"That's exactly what I'm afraid to do around you," she said, shoulders slumping. "Talk too much."

And with a regretful glance at him, Rachel left, heading toward her group of friends waiting near the hall's entrance.

All Ian could do was watch her go, because he wasn't going to chase after her. Nope.

Maybe he'd lost most of his edge, but he sure as hell wasn't going to lose *himself* in the same bargain.

Chapter Five

If Friday's hearing had gone badly, today's hearing was redefining the description.

President Alex Broadstreet had gotten past the "praise Gilbert" phase and was questioning a crusading Nate Williams, who was drawing on all his power as one of the top criminal-defense attorneys in the state.

Not that it was intimidating Broadstreet, Rachel thought, wrapping her large sweater over the front of her body.

She exhaled the breath she'd been holding, her eyes meeting Ian's from where he stood near the front of the hall. He held his notepad and pen at the ready, his gaze digging into her.

A shock tore through Rachel, and she immediately put all of her effort into avoiding him. How was she supposed to interpret his explanations about this morning's article? Sure, he'd faulted his editor for the salacious tone, but did that mean she could trust him?

Did she even *believe* Ian?

Broadstreet's voice filtered over her misgivings.

"Mr. Williams, aren't you the last person who should have shown up here to defend Professor Harrison?" He leaned over the table on his forearms, as if ready to pounce.

With a glower, Nate engaged his foe. He angled forward, as well, meeting the other man's glare with laser intensity. "I should think I'd be the first person to come to Gilbert's aid, with all he's done for me."

The president played with a pen, twining it through the fingers of one hand, hotdogging before making his point. "Can you tell us anything about grade changing?"

Broadstreet had, at some point, managed to hint about this subject during the two previous testimonials. Although Nate's composure didn't wane at the question, Gilbert's did. The professor took a deeper breath than usual, his face going red.

He sure as fire looked guilty. But…no. He wouldn't have done something like *this*. Right?

Rachel cringed.

Deep in her heart, she knew that if Gilbert had changed Nate's grades, he'd only done it to give the promising student a second chance during the worst point in his life. Yet the accusation sounded so awful coming from Broadstreet.

The president stood, took a few steps closer to Gilbert's chair. "You have something to say, Mr. Harrison?"

Gilbert's skin turned even redder. "I—"

Nate interrupted. "*Professor* Harrison tutored me, giving me a chance to earn those marks on my own merit. It was due to the self-esteem Gilbert instilled in me that I even had a shot in life."

What was he saying? He wasn't denying that Gilbert *had* done it. Rachel knew that Nate was embarking on a new life with Kathryn and that he had promised to never lie again since the past was full of too many destructive secrets.

Was he trying to dance around the subject while avoiding the need to fib?

And why wasn't Gilbert defending himself if he was innocent?

"Self-esteem," Broadstreet repeated, shaking his head. "How *Gilbert*."

Within moments, the attorney offered his own smile to Broadstreet, a definite serving of polite sarcasm. Calmly, he reclined in his chair, steepled his hands on the table.

"If Saunders intends to create the best citizens possible, the most well-rounded human beings, then your outdated, assembly-line philosophy needs to change, Mr. Broadstreet."

"It's *President* B—"

Nate charged ahead, putting Broadstreet on the defensive. "When I got into this college, I became a real piece of work. Gilbert and his self-esteem were the only things that kept me sane."

"And now we come down to it." Broadstreet didn't skip a beat, didn't allow any pause that could encourage sympathy for the attorney. "I'm guessing this is the part where we hear about how Harrison changed your life and you ultimately made the world a better place. Yes?"

Surprisingly, all Nate did was shoot a concerned glance to Gilbert as the president continued.

"You don't exactly stand up for the 'little guys' or petition for the betterment of humankind, Mr. Williams. In fact, you've represented rapists and drug dealers to secure major fame and fortune. How can you sit here and justify Gilbert Harrison's tactics when you haven't done society a bit of good?"

"I'm working on that part, Mr. Broadstreet," Nate said softly.

And Rachel knew it was true. Her boss wasn't a terrible man. His intellect had given him the opportunity to earn a lot of money, and he had taken it—the easy road. He was only human, but she knew he aspired to be more.

Broadstreet allowed Gilbert to respond to this latest testimony, but the professor's vague comments—along with Nate's damage control—didn't seem to matter. Once again, the president had plucked the worst out of the best and come out the victor.

And Rachel wasn't the only one who thought so. The moment a break was announced, Sandra Westport leaned over to her friend.

"Do you think Gilbert really changed Nate's grades?" she asked.

Once again, Rachel recalled her adoption papers and she hastily changed the subject. "I don't know. But why isn't he speaking up? He could defend himself much better, Sandra."

They were both silent while they watched the crowd mingle around them. Broadstreet looked very self-satisfied as he drank coffee and ate pastries with his comrades. Ian Beck huddled over his notes, and when his photographer returned, they both munched on what looked to be sandwiches from a snack cart. Ella Gardner and Cassidy Maxwell swooped over to Gilbert before anyone else could get there and guided him outside, engaging him in a conversation that seemed to heat up by the second.

"It's not going to do any good," Sandra said.

"I can't imagine a reason strong enough to keep his mouth closed during all this—his crucifixion."

"That's the truth. And we're getting hammered from all sides. I saw Ian Beck's article."

"I gave the guy hell about that." Rachel repeated Ian's explanation about his marauding editor. "I want to believe him, but…"

"You make it sound like Beck's on our side," Sandra said, glancing curiously at Rachel.

Tired of hiding it, she sighed. "He is. At least, that's what I thought."

Rachel finally explained everything—the truth about her connection to the reporter, what she'd been trying so very hard to do for Gilbert's reputation.

In the end, Sandra agreed with Rachel's philosophy. Hopefully the rest of the group would understand just as easily.

Hopefully.

"Really, I wouldn't be surprised if Beck's boss really did fiddle with the article. I hear that sort of thing happens. I've been lucky on my own paper, though."

True enough, Rachel thought. Sandra was a local reporter, so she knew the drill. Her acceptance of Ian's excuse put a little faith back into her heart.

But not a lot.

"Too bad you're not on the story," Rachel said. "Maybe then we'd get good coverage."

"Conflict of interest. But you know the worst part?"

"It gets worse?"

"You bet, because after today, your friend Ian Beck isn't going to need an editor to make mincemeat out of Gilbert."

Rachel sighed and drew her bundled coat close to her belly, comforted, as if the material was a security blanket.

"Broadstreet is doing a great job of that on his own," she said.

And the trend continued as Dr. Jacob Weber testified.

* * *

After the hearing finished for the day, Ian reluctantly left Rachel with her distraught friends and settled under an oak tree near Lumley Hall with his laptop, itching to write his rough draft.

The words seemed to fly from his fingertips, straight onto the screen. First, the tale of Nate Williams's unsuccessful testimony. Then of Jacob Weber's.

He was supposed to be the cavalry, the answer to the damage Nate Williams had brought to the proceedings. But when Dr. Jacob Weber stepped up to the table, he didn't have a chance.

Ian paused, setting up the scene in his mind, consulting his notes sporadically, even though every moment was etched into his memory.

This was a man with a former reputation for nastiness and arrogance, a renowned fertility specialist who'd done right by Professor Harrison as far as success goes. He was a ringer for Harrison's cause. But not today.
Not with President Broadstreet on a roll.
After laying the foundation of his argument with Weber's history of violence on campus, Broadstreet then went on to question how Gilbert Harrison could say he had "done some good" for the

students with his unorthodox counseling methods if Weber was prone to such behavior. [insert salacious details here]

Immediately, Ian hit the backspace button, erasing the bracketed note. Screw Edgar the Editor. The last thing Rachel...or rather, Gilbert, that's right, *Gilbert*... needed was negativity.

Even though that's what today's hearing had been all about. In fact, Ian *himself* was at the point where he was wondering if Professor Harrison was guilty of Broadstreet's charges.

He exhaled, then went back to it.

Even as Weber fought his temper, he composed himself enough to give his favorite teacher glowing reviews, insisting that Harrison is a pillar of Saunders University and that he deserves the chance to help more students. [insert quotes and color here]
Yet in spite of his best efforts, Weber failed to convince a hushed audience. In fact, a smirking Alex Broadstreet even had the temerity to cut the doctor's testimony short, citing the need to attend important meetings.
Due to these overwhelmingly urgent plans, Broadstreet then announced that the hearing would continue the day after tomorrow, when his agenda could accommodate it....

Crap.

Out of sheer frustration, Ian deleted what he'd written so far.

It was crap. Biased. A damn sight short of his usual prose.

What was with him?

Good God, why even ask. Ian knew what was chapping his hide.

His heart wasn't in this story—not with the way it was going for Gilbert and the woman Ian had come to care about more than he wanted to admit.

As he closed up his computer, he wondered if he could get away with deserting this story, leaving it for another reporter to cover with his own uninspired writing. But that wasn't his style—to leave something hanging on a job.

No, that was left to the other areas of his life, where coming and going were second nature.

He sat back in the chilled breeze, trying to get a grip on his fire. His damned *edge.* But neither of them were anywhere handy.

Even though he knew he'd end up writing the article using the facts, he didn't feel great about it.

But right now, all his questions were centering around how he could help Professor Harrison, and that wasn't good.

Not for a reporter, anyway.

It's just the surface. Dig more, his instincts told him. *Find that hero you want to uncover.*

Discover what he's hiding.

When Ian saw Rachel slipping out of Lumley Hall, he didn't waste any more time.

With a burst of energy, he bolted toward her, intending to head her off before she left campus.

Minutes later, he did, catching up with her near the little red-brick theater.

"Not so fast," he said, gently grabbing her arm with one hand, his laptop tucked haphazardly under the other arm.

She was wearing that same threadbare coat, coupled with a long wool skirt and boots. The outfit all but swallowed her whole, scratching at Ian's heart because every clue indicated that she couldn't afford any better.

"Ian." Her gaze was dark with exhaustion. "Now's not a good time."

"When is?" Steeling himself for a rejection, he gripped her other arm, making sure she faced him. Then he bent a little lower so they were eye to eye—so he could glance at her straight on and show her how much he wanted to help.

When she sighed, he realized that she was weak and unsteady.

"Did you have any lunch?"

"Sandra and I talked through the break."

"Dammit, Rachel."

He steered her toward a snack cart, buying her a bottle of apple juice and a hot dog.

"But…"

"My treat," he said.

She flushed but thanked him gracefully.

He played it off, her gratitude making him feel more heroic than he should, for some reason.

"Man," he said, "it's cold. Let's go inside."

They ended up in the theater's modest lobby, with its gold curtains, closed box office and tiled floor. A blast of heat greeted them as they claimed a waiting bench. Framed posters of *Tartuffe,* the most recent production, added flair to an otherwise quiet space.

As she nibbled at the hot dog, he took off his jacket, revealing the crewneck sweater he wore underneath.

"You need to take better care of yourself," he said.

"Thanks, Lunch Monitor." A spot of mustard lingered near the tip of her mouth as she risked a smile.

Before he could think, Ian reached out, thumbed the mustard away. Rachel gulped down the food in her mouth.

He felt a little weird, too, so he hunkered down, forearms on his lower thighs.

Come on, shrug it off, he told himself. *What's with you?*

"What did you think of the facts today?" he asked.

She drank some juice. "Pretty awful. Gilbert's coming off in a bad way."

"That's what I thought. What kind of article would you write for tomorrow's paper?"

"The same one you're probably going to."

The resulting pause hushed through the lobby, thick as the morning fog.

"It doesn't have to be that way," he finally said, giving voice to what he felt in his gut.

The doubt.

The instinct shouting that there was a lot Gilbert wasn't telling them.

Rachel's hand brushed his sweater. "What do you mean, 'It doesn't have to be that way'?"

He couldn't answer for a moment, because there was a flare of warmth blazing over his skin, a sensual heaviness under the bit of wool where Rachel had touched him.

It was hard to get his mind back on work, but he managed. "I know something's going on, Rachel. All these strange glances everyone is exchanging, all the tension between you and Gilbert and your friends… If someone would just talk, things might not turn out so terrible. I'm going to uncover it in my research, anyway."

Famous last words.

She was biting her lip, as if forcibly restraining a comment.

"Rachel, please… Give me a reason to let the guy off the hook. *Please.* I can't make excuses for Gilbert, even if I want to see him pull through all this garbage."

"I can't."

"Why not?" Ian sat up, bringing his face dangerously close to hers.

Those eyes—like strong coffee from the Moroccan cafés he had frequented during his travels.

Those lips—full and pink and soft.

"Because," she whispered, "I'm afraid to tell you any more than you already know."

"You don't trust me."

She hesitated, and he inched nearer to her.

That perfume—soft jasmine wafting out of a shaded shop in an exotic bazaar.

Before he could stop himself, he leaned forward, giving in, skimming his lips over hers, breathing over the plump moistness of them. He felt, more than heard, her quick intake of air.

"Trust me, Rachel," he whispered.

Her wide-eyed pause was excruciating—a heartbeat paused in its pattering rhythm.

But then, with a tiny gasp, she pressed her mouth against his, giving him a taste of her: sharp mustard and sweet ketchup, a hint of apple. He sucked at her mouth, drawing in her essence, his body demanding more.

And he took it, true to his yearnings, gathering her in his arms and pulling her close, slipping his hands under her coat to caress her back, to press her against his chest.

Her sweater rubbed against his, causing warm friction, heat. Her breasts were small but full, and he longed to take them in his palms, memorize them.

But instead he waited…agonizing moments, body-pulsing possibilities.

As their kiss deepened, she relaxed, threaded her fingers through his hair, cupping the back of his head.

Ian felt the first wave of dizziness wrap around his brain, buzz through his body, taunt him with questions…too many questions.

Who was this woman?

How could she be controlling him like this, with just one kiss?

Maybe she was asking similar things because, before he knew it, she was hitching in a breath, disengaging and leaning her forehead against his.

"Nice interviewing technique," she whispered.

He laughed, taken aback by her joke. He'd expected denial from her, maybe embarrassment.

"I do what I have to."

Silence swallowed them. Was she wondering if he'd kissed her for that very reason? The pursuit of a story?

"I'm kidding," he added.

Smiling, she backed away, closing up her coat and clearing her throat. "I know. Heck, I was even wondering if kissing would help to divert you. But I imagine working my wiles will have no effect."

He wasn't so sure about that.

She continued, a hint of heartbreaking hope on her face. "But, tell me, anyway. What *would* make you stop writing about Gilbert?"

He must've seemed shocked, because she corrected herself.

"No. Not *that*. I wasn't… I wouldn't…"

"Got it." He took one of her hands in his. "You're not that type of woman."

She sagged with obvious relief and glanced down at their connected hands, clearly enjoying his gesture as she entwined her fingers with his. "I'm such a goof."

"No, you're not. You just care about Gilbert."

"He's the only person who's ever given uncondi- tionally to me. I don't like to see him hurt—by Broad- street *or* by you."

The weight of expectation settled on his chest. Maybe she was hoping that he would abandon the story, too.

"The truth," Ian said, "is the truth. You can't get around it…unless there's more than meets the eye in Gilbert's case."

There. He'd given her another shot to come clean. And from the indecision on her face, he was near to get- ting some kind of confession.

But she was a tough one, all right. She didn't say a word.

God, maybe he was a dreamer. Could it be that Gilbert Harrison was an overconfident lout who really did take advantage of students in his office while he pol- ished his image by helping others?

Reluctantly, Ian squeezed her hand and let go. Then he started to put his coat back on. "Okay, then. I guess that's it."

"What's it?"

"Gilbert is what he seems, I suppose. But I'm not surprised. Even good people have dark sides, Rachel, and it could be that Gilbert's is finally being exposed."

"That's not true. That's not…"

There she went again, looking confused and lost.

Ian helped her off the seat. She stood in front of him, not meeting his gaze.

"Can't you admit the worst about your adored Gilbert?" he asked. "Can't you even consider the question?"

Why did all of this sound ridiculous, even to him?

What was it about Gilbert that made him want to so desperately *believe?*

"Ian," she said, seeming sadder than ever, "I've considered the question of his innocence. I really have."

"Then talk to me. Let me in on what you're thinking. You could be holding the key to clearing his name, Rachel, and you might not even know it."

She tossed her hot dog wrapping into a garbage container, then walked toward the glass door. "Let me think about it, okay? Let me…I don't know…run it past my friends. It's about time I did that. If I…"

By now he thought he knew Rachel well enough to finish that sentence for her.

If I have the courage.

She knew something, all right. Ian would bet his left leg on it.

But before he could say anything more, she thanked him again for the hot dog and left.

He watched her through the glass, and when she lifted her hand up to her lips, as if testing the memory of their kiss, his pulse gave a jolt.

Get off it, he told himself. *It's not like your kiss is the secret to unlocking her.*

But he could hope, couldn't he?

Chapter Six

At loose ends, Rachel had called a few select friends for a meeting, but all four of them were unable to gather as a group until the next afternoon.

As they came together around a back-room table at Brewster's, the dark tavern located near campus, Rachel knew she was about to discover if everyone—including herself—would fully accept Ian as an ally.

Even after the latest article that had come out this morning.

This second story had made Gilbert out to be a shady character, too, except that, this time, Ian's editor hadn't needed to alter the presentation.

After Rachel greeted everyone—Cassidy, Jane and Ella—they ordered a round of drinks and made small talk, enjoying the relative quiet of a little nook the owner had reserved for them. As she'd done earlier, she made an ice-breaking joke about how they'd set her up for breakfast with Gilbert, just to show she appreciated their concern.

When the beverages arrived, Rachel sipped at her cinnamon apple cider, chasing away the catch in her throat as well as a lingering disappointment in Ian. She couldn't fault him for doing his job, yet she still couldn't help feeling betrayed: Ian was harming Gilbert, a man who had been the closest thing she'd ever had to a father.

And she couldn't forget that.

She also couldn't forget what else had happened between her and the reporter yesterday. That kiss. A knock-me-dead-on-the-floor touch of the lips that was causing her legs to go rubbery even now.

Did she trust him? Or was he playing games with her, even now?

She'd yearned for input from some of the people who'd come to know her the best.

Cassidy Maxwell, the ambassador's assistant whom Rachel respected greatly, spoke first. "You all set for tomorrow, Rach?"

Ba-boom went her thundering, stressed-out heart. "I'm going to do whatever I can for Gilbert."

Auburn-haired Cassidy patted Rachel's shoulder. "We'll do fine up there."

"*You'll* be great," Rachel said, as impressed as always by Cassidy's sophistication, by the way she could command a room just by stepping into it. "But as for my grace under fire? No way."

Today at work, Nate had spent a few hours coaching her. Sure, it'd increased her self-esteem, but it didn't erase any worries about Broadstreet and his vendetta.

"Just pretend the jerk is in his underwear," said Jane Jackson, winking at Rachel.

"Yeah." Ella's blond Shirley Temple-ish curls bobbed as she nodded, warming to the idea. "And imagine that the jerk has R2-D2 and C-3PO all over his boxers. He's got to have *a few* good qualities, like maybe a sense of humor."

"Somewhere," Jane said.

"Deeply hidden," Cassidy added.

That was the cue for everyone to express their doubt with animated comments, but in spite of the verve, a pause ultimately came between them, filled only by the sipping of their drinks.

Putting down hers, Rachel took a deep breath, finally warmed up and ready to get down to the meat of the matter. "I know we've addressed this to the point of tearing our hair out, but Gilbert's at a dangerous point here. I feel like the only way we're going to help him is by coming clean about everything. And I'm talking about all these secrets that are flying around. Things we aren't even sharing with one another."

Jane slid Rachel a look that clearly stated, "Are you saying that you'll share first?"

God, how she wanted to tell them about Gilbert's

possession of the adoption documents. With every day
that passed, the urge to share buried Rachel under pressure, alienated her to the point of feeling fifteen years
old again, afraid and alone. Her friends knew she was
adopted, but how would they react to Gilbert's strange
interest in her past?

"Are you referring to what we found in the safe?"
Jane asked.

Rachel swallowed. "Maybe not all of the information."

Chicken.

They all exchanged a look. Rachel knew they hadn't
invaded her privacy by glancing at the sealed papers.
Yet she knew they were anxious to hear what was bothering Rachel and eager to air out everyone's problems
once and for all.

Especially since Rachel wasn't the only one who'd
had files tucked away in Gilbert's safe.

Yet, even though Rachel wondered what her friends
were hiding themselves, she didn't dare ask, realizing
it wasn't her business to know. Realizing that she
couldn't share her own secrets, after all.

Ella stirred her cola with a straw. "I know we said
that this is a last resort, but…"

"The benefactor," Jane finished for her.

They all took that in for a moment. Ella and Jacob
had already informed the gang—minus the withdrawn
Rachel—that Gilbert was the anonymous benefactor on
the Saunders campus. And when the Westports had at-

tempted to tell Rachel at dinner one night, she'd been so skittish about her own secret that she'd left before they could reveal anything. However, Sandra had made up for it, along with Jane, finally catching Rachel and disclosing what was going on.

Jane ran a hand over her face, sighing. "As Ella said before, Gilbert kept his status as the benefactor silent for a reason. I have no idea what it might be, but he's been stubborn about coming clean about this, even if his good works could clear him."

"I still think that *he* should be the one to announce it," Ella added.

Rachel wanted to pound the table with her fists. "Why are we even debating again? That's all we do. You all have seen what's happening with Alex Broadstreet. He's killing Gilbert in the hearing."

"Believe me," Ella said, "I've been trying to convince Gilbert, but he's having none of it. He still thinks nobody in our group knows and that he's going to keep this under wraps forever. No amount of wheedling can convince him to be honest."

Cassidy shook her head. "He's scared, afraid that his string-pulling could lose him a job that he's held for thirty-one years, a job that's filled his life with utter joy." She paused, flashed a glance to Rachel, then fiddled with her soda glass. "He's terrified of a lot of things."

The comment rattled Rachel. Was Cassidy referring to Rachel's own documents? No. How many times did she have to remind herself that her friends wouldn't have looked at those? So how would Cassidy…?

Great. Rachel was paranoid. There was no reason to fly off the handle here.

Still, this was the opening she'd been waiting for. She could tell her friends what Gilbert had been secreting in that safe, could tell them how shocked she was, how confused.

But Rachel couldn't say a word. Maybe it was because giving voice to her puzzlement would make it too real, would force her into taking action—something she'd been scared to death of doing since she was a kid.

"So what's the bottom line?" Jane asked. "What do we do?"

"I still vote that we respect Gilbert's privacy and keep the truth to ourselves," Ella said. "He wouldn't appreciate us taking matters into our own hands, and telling him would just give him more to worry about. Our respect means the world to him, and if he thinks he's lost it because he was lying…"

This seemed to decide matters. Thus, one by one, they all vowed to stay true to Gilbert's wishes. Yet the promise tore through Rachel, because she knew it was wrong.

But then again, what was right these days? She couldn't even be sure anymore.

"Then I've got a plan B," Rachel said, drawing their pleasantly surprised attention. Her heart warmed at their expressions, their joy at having her back in the inner circle.

"I've been talking with Ian Beck…"

Much to Rachel's relief, her friends merely nodded, hardly passing the fire-and-brimstone judgement she'd feared.

Cassidy patted Rachel's hand. "Sandra told us."

"Then you'll understand why I want to talk to him again," she said. "I'd like to give him most of the nitty-gritty personal details I've been holding back." Except for the one she couldn't even tell her friends about. "I'm going to get the press and the community on our side by finally telling my own story."

"Rachel," Jane asked, "you trust him that much?"

"I don't know." She got out her cell phone, wondering if this wasn't so much a matter of trust as much as a matter of also trying to throw him off the scent of the benefactor story. "But it's the only thing I can think of doing right now."

Thus, Rachel dialed Ian's number, pulse skittering.

Beating in desperate time.

That evening, Ian was able to meet Rachel in front of the Old State House, a red-brick landmark that had formerly served as the seat of the colonial government.

He had wanted to get a picture of the Red Sox bunny in front of the historical building for his nieces and nephews, then send it via e-mail to their correspondence loop.

As he spotted Rachel coming toward him, he noted the cute flush to her cheeks, the chill of a cold night.

When she'd called him to request a meeting, he'd been oddly ecstatic.

But he'd met women in casual circumstances before. So why was he acting like this was the first time?

Was this too much like a date even though it was a nonevent?

They greeted each other, and he held out the bunny. "Do me a favor?" he asked.

"Only if you grant me one later."

His blood thudded, sending zings of anticipation down to his groin.

Down, boy, down.

He cleared his throat, hoping his voice wouldn't go all adolescent and squeaky, betraying his excitement. "Take Mr. Bunny Man for a second and hold him up in front of the building? I want to record this part of my trip for posterity. And, please. Make him look like he's having fun, okay?"

As he grinned and took a digital camera out of his jacket pocket, she positioned herself and the little stuffed animal before the lens, taking care to keep herself out of the photo.

But sneaky him. Ian focused so that she was in the frame. The kids would ask who she was and his brothers and sisters-in-law would go nuts, but he wanted Rachel in his mementos. Strange, but true.

What was happening to him, he didn't know. But he wasn't ashamed about the way he was starting to feel about her. No, he was just wary of the trouble he could get into with such a tempting woman. A woman who deserved a lot more than his free-as-a-bird lifestyle could offer.

As he snapped away, he talked, noticing how photogenic she was with that thick, gorgeous dark hair, her wide brown eyes, the classic shape of her face.

"The Old State House," he said. "Location of the Boston Massacre."

"Are you going to relate all the gory details in your e-mail to the kids?"

"I'll go easy on them, even though some of my guys and girls are old enough to have already learned about Crispus Attucks and the bloody night of 1770."

When he finished, Rachel teasingly petted the bunny, then handed it to him. With care, he wrapped it back up in its bag and secured it in his pocket again.

"You must be the cool uncle," she said as they started walking away from the building, tacitly agreeing to find someplace warmer. "Uncle World Traveler. Do the kids worship you or what?"

"Of course." He shot her a cocky grin. "But I think it has something to do with the candy I bring."

They were headed for a bookstore, a charming spot that looked like the kind of place Ben Franklin or Thomas Jefferson would've enjoyed. He could see shelves of hardbound volumes through the window, dark wood, potted plants and the mellow glow of soft lights.

She noticed his curious assessment. "When I asked you to meet me, it wasn't just a social call."

His heart rolled over and played dead, or at least that's what it felt like. Here he'd been replaying yesterday's kiss in his mind, wondering if she wanted to take things a step further by seeing him tonight.

Ian, my boy, he thought, *you're still thinking like a guy who mingles with women who are as eager for instant companionship as you. Rachel James isn't that way. Get used to it.*

"What did you have in mind, then?" he asked.

"An interview."

With that, she opened the bookstore's glass door, a hopeful expression making him a little weak in the knees.

Good God.

He took the door from Rachel and waited for her to precede him. They were greeted by a Mozart requiem, the scent of yellowed pages, timeworn leather and old wood.

With a nod at the male owner, who stood behind the counter wearing square-lensed glasses and a fuzzy green sweater with snowflakes on it, Rachel led Ian toward the back of the empty store. A fire snapped in its grate, lending illumination to the overstuffed couches and chairs.

"I come here a lot," she said as they took off their jacket and coat. "Secondhand books. Isaac used to drop me off when he'd go down the block to a tavern for Sunday football with the guys. Now I swing by after work sometimes, just to feel like I'm around something, even if it's only books." She laughed, surveying the cozy area. "I'm not sure I've ever finished a novel I bought here, though."

He could tell she was holding a lot of things back, in spite of her smile. Was she in a good mood because she was glad to be around him?

Or was he totally going haywire in the head?

"So," he said, settling back in his chair, "an interview."

"Yeah. I've enlightened you about Gilbert before but…"

"You've never gotten too personal about yourself or how he's affected you beyond the general."

She stared into the fire. "I was kind of hoping you could put something together, the kind of article you were wishing for. One that shows how much we all love Gilbert and how lucky Saunders is to have him."

A community piece, Ian thought. *A story with heart and heat.* With the superficial negativity of his articles so far, the idea of balancing his coverage with some humanistic, positive angles sounded right on.

"I've already turned in my ink for tomorrow's paper," he said. "Student reactions to Nate's and Jacob's testimonies. Gilbert will get some good press from that because the kids were pretty supportive."

"But I'm testifying tomorrow," she said, meeting his gaze head-on. "Would your audience be interested in peeking behind the scenes, finding out how Gilbert helped out one ex-student in particular?"

Oh, yeah, he thought. It sounded perfect, touching. A piece that could run in *Newsweek* or *Time*. He could do wonders with Rachel.

At the same time, though, he wished his ambition would shut down. He longed to have her tell him everything about herself because she wanted to, not because she had to.

But…hell. Who was he to squander this opportunity?

And who was he to think there could be something that went beyond this story with her?

Without a second thought, he eased his notepad out of his other pocket. "What do you want to tell me, Rachel?"

"Every last secret." She grinned, the gesture wry and self-aware. "Or, at least I'll come as close as I can get, okay?"

"Anytime you're ready."

And he meant that in so many ways.

She leaned back in her own chair, propping her elbow on the armrest, cradling her head in a palm as she watched him.

For a moment, Ian took her in, caught by her beauty. Snared by the want of her.

"I've already told you that I'm adopted," she began. "From what my parents said, they believed there would be no natural children in their future. It was a closed adoption, and I was just a baby, only weeks old." She sighed. "My dad used to tell me that he and Mom were 'enchanted' by me at first. My mom just used to say that they wanted to raise a new kid before anyone else could teach them bad habits and I was the latest arrival."

Ian looked up from his scribbling, forehead furrowed. "Sounds like a love match."

"At the beginning, it was close, I suppose. My skin was darker then. But over the first years I lost that tone and it was obvious that I wasn't exactly like them."

Trouble ahead, Ian thought. He could detect the seeds of it already.

"When did you find out you were adopted?" he asked.

"I don't know the exact age, but it was as soon as I could understand the concept. I know they were just trying to be good parents by being honest with me about that, but it caused a real rift, a distance that only got worse and worse. I think we all become painfully aware that I didn't belong with them. I felt like I wasn't all theirs, and when things got rough, I would get into trouble, get punished, then retreat into these fantasies about my real parents."

"Did you ever try to find them?"

"No." Her answer was quick. Too quick.

He was almost afraid to ask why, because Rachel suddenly seemed so fragile. All he wanted to do was help her to keep it together, to be the glue for her, because he knew that she had strength. He'd seen it in the way she interacted with him.

"I…" She looked into his eyes. Then, miraculously, she seemed to get the message, his fervent wish that she would believe in herself a little more.

That's when Rachel straightened up on the couch, chin lifting a little higher. Affection drilled near his heart, seeking a way in.

And succeeding all too easily.

"For years," she said, "I've wanted to find my birth parents but…well, truthfully…I've been so afraid. Terrified of what I might find out about them or, God forbid, of why they had to give me up. I wasn't sure I could take all the rejection, so I stuck with what I knew and never searched. Not that it would be easy with the closed adoption."

"Rachel, they probably had good reason to give you up. If they saw you, they'd…" What? Love her with all the emotion she'd been missing from her adoptive parents?

Who could help but to adore her?

Ian took a second to mark on his notepad, getting as far away from that line of thinking as he could. "You mentioned a sister?"

"A miracle baby." The ghost of a smile touched Rachel's lips. "Jeanne. No one expected her, but there she was. Beautiful, so tiny and perfect. She looked just like my adoptive parents."

Rachel choked to a stop.

"You don't have to go on," Ian said. But, dammit, he wanted to know, wanted to share everything with her because a simple guy like him—one with a family he'd never trade in, one who'd lived a carefree, full life up until this point—could help.

He could make her feel so much better.

Holding up a finger, Rachel told him that she *would* continue.

Just as he knew she could.

"After Jeanne came to us," she finally said, voice quivering slightly, "things got tense. It's like my parents wanted to punish me for existing and taking up the time and money they could have been spending on Jeanne. They didn't have a lot of either one, what, with Mom working and taking care of us and Dad holding down two jobs. I think they regretted ever taking me in at that point. I started being punished for the smallest things. Anything I cleaned wasn't spotless enough, anything I cooked tasted terrible. They accused me of taking kitchen supplies and hiding them in my room, too, so then they thought of a new punishment: they would show me the table of food the family would eat for dinner and then tell me I wasn't good enough to deserve any of it."

Instinctively, Ian ran a gaze over Rachel's shapeless skirt and sweater, noting once again that she was too thin. "They starved you?"

"Not starved, no. They gave me regular meals between punishments and, honestly, it didn't happen all the time. And I was rebellious, so it could be that I brought on their anger. But they always apologized and promised a fresh start between us. Still, I never forgot the feeling of being unworthy, the guilt of eating more than I need to, the things they said to me out of anger— things they might not have meant."

Memories rushed him: Rachel refusing food at the Thai restaurant. Rachel skipping lunch at the hearing.

Rachel's loose clothing.

"And school wasn't much better in the comfort department," she added, playing with the hem of her sweater as if she knew what Ian was thinking. "Where we lived, there were definite distinctions based on skin color. Kids had attitude about people who were too dark or too light. As usual, I fell somewhere in between two ethnicities, so… Well, I guess I withdrew, went into my own little world where my real parents had hung on to me and I had lots of friends. I fell in with the misfits at lunchtime, a group that had their own culture and didn't conform to 'black' or 'white' or 'any of the above'."

Ian was beginning to anticipate how Gilbert, her guidance counselor, had fit into Rachel's life, even before she continued.

"As you can guess, my grades were terrible, but when I hit high school, something happened. I joined every club and activity and started to get popular. Maybe it was because I pretended to be happy and everyone was attracted to that. You know how teenagers are—they hate themselves more than anybody else and are drawn to people who don't seem to fall into that trap. I was good at pretending. I mean, heck, I was president of the Drama Club. Those were great days for me. I was finally accepted."

"You became a normal all-American Girl?"

"On the outside. But I wasn't comfortable with myself, and that showed with boys."

Ian's ears perked right up.

Rachel laughed. "You knew I'd get around to this part."

"I was kinda hoping."

She blushed and shyly glanced away. "I never allowed moss to grow on any relationship because I thought that whoever I grew attached to would leave me before I could leave them. That's what you get when you're adopted, I guess. A raging lonely complex. Gilbert saw the pattern in college, and he worked with me to overcome it. But then I met Isaac, an older man with a lot of charisma, and I thought I'd cured myself. And maybe I did. We lived with each other for five wonderful years."

Ian didn't want to hear about this so much. He didn't want to picture Rachel in someone else's arms. It just...

His body tensed at the thought.

"So," she said, clearly unaware of his fruitless battle, "I had the bad grades going, and that didn't surprise me. My adoptive parents sometimes told me I was dumb, and I believed it, even if they would contradict themselves a couple days down the road."

"If I ever meet them..."

He stopped himself. Rachel's eyes had widened, as if she couldn't believe he was thinking that far ahead.

"We don't keep in contact," she said.

"It's still not right," Ian added, explaining his outburst. When she smiled at him, he eased up, almost glad he'd gone over the edge and revealed more than he should have to her. Almost.

Because Ian was flailing here, falling faster and faster....

"And here we come to the real point of the story." She smoothed out her skirt. "Gilbert. I needed to get out of the house, so I applied to every college in Massachusetts, I think. I even had to get a part-time job as a waitress to pay for the application fees, but it was so worth it. One university made me an offer and, after I turned them down, they offered this great financial-aid package. So I accepted. That brought me to Saunders, where I met Gilbert."

"I thought your grades were poor," Ian said, recalling the same thing about David Westport's high school marks, wondering why Saunders had accepted her.

"They were, but they seemed to want me. Probably because of affirmative action, I guess."

She didn't seem any more convinced than he did as they shared a look that spoke volumes. Ian was hard-pressed to translate exactly what was happening between them. Maybe it was about the story. Maybe it was something more.

Something Ian wanted—and didn't want—to acknowledge.

"Gilbert," she said, "helped me through everything from a social life to academics. See, I liked to quit both things when the going got rough, and he discouraged me from doing that. It was funny, but Gilbert was the one who finally showed me affection, and I grew so much from that. And then I met Isaac during my junior year."

Once again, Ian bristled.

"Personally," she continued, "I was stronger than I'd ever been, but my grades were still the pits. When Isaac and I started dating, things really took off for us. He was such a good man, so handsome. Big and protective. I felt lucky to have found someone who said I was wonderful and listened to every word I said as if they were jewels. I ended up marrying him, quitting college and getting a job, since Isaac wasn't exactly rich. Neither of us were, but that didn't matter. We were in love. Gilbert didn't react well. He was wounded, and I think he felt betrayed because he'd put so much time into making me believe that I could finish my education and get a great job. He tried really hard to keep me on campus, but I was set in my ways. So I left."

"And lived...?" Happily ever after? Nope. Ian already knew the sad ending to this tale.

"You know enough to fill in the blanks," Rachel said. "If I had listened to Gilbert and graduated from Saunders during my marriage, I might be another Cassidy Maxwell or Nate Williams. It's my fault Isaac and I had money troubles, because Gilbert showed me a way to avoid that. I could've stayed in school or... God, what was I thinking?"

"What matters the most," he said, "is that you came back for Gilbert when he needed you."

"He's been having a tough time this year. Besides, I

thought spending more time with him again would bring back the optimism he'd started up in me. I thought that, maybe, I could find the courage from him to get my life back in order. To search for my real parents, but then I found some papers…"

It was as if a shield had slammed down over her.

"What?" Ian asked.

She hesitated, the muscles in her jaw working as she stared into the fire.

He knew she'd slipped away. It was in the way she'd barricaded herself, retreated into her own private safety zone once again.

"Do you have enough to go on now?" she asked, standing, fidgeting with her skirt. He'd never seen someone who wanted to escape so badly.

"Maybe we can talk more later," he offered, hoping she'd agree, dreading that she wouldn't.

"Yeah. Later. But for now…" She smiled at him, an apology, a plea for understanding. "Rain check?"

He tried to be casual, as if he wouldn't go back to his hotel room and lie awake in his bed all night, thinking of her. "You've got a big day tomorrow with testifying."

"I sure do."

Don't let her go, he thought. Just one more minute, one more hour…

"Need an escort back to your place?"

She must've picked up on his need to stay with her, because the planes of her face softened, reflecting what he was feeling, too.

Sheer hunger. A longing for someone to talk to, to touch.

"I really need to go," she said. "Thank you, though. For everything."

After she gave him a reluctant wave, he watched her leave, the knowledge that he'd see her at the hearing tomorrow hardly assuaging him.

Because it was an eternity away.

An endless night of wanting her.

Chapter Seven

As soon as Cassidy Maxwell finished testifying, a collective, celebratory *whoop!* filled Lumley Hall.

Eric Barnes was the first to rush up to her and Gilbert, but Rachel brought up a close second.

"You did it!" Eric said, enclosing his girlfriend in an exuberant hug.

The strong and silent type, Cassidy nevertheless broke into a huge smile and returned Eric's affection as their group gathered around, patting her back and offering congratulations.

Rachel couldn't help riding cloud nine, especially when Gilbert started embracing his ex-students one by one.

When he got to Rachel, he held her at arm's length. "Finally," he said, "Alex Broadstreet is thwarted."

As the professor hugged her, she closed her eyes, reveling in the hope of healing what was between her and Gilbert.

Yet when Rachel opened her gaze, she found Broadstreet glaring at them, straightening his papers.

His notes for Rachel, no doubt.

With a spike of adrenaline, she remembered she was next, and now that Cassidy had expertly turned Gilbert's prospects around for the better, Rachel imagined that the president would be doubling his efforts.

Shaken, Rachel turned to Cassidy. The unflappable woman worked with global leaders and politicians on a frequent basis, and her talent for putting people in their places with her quiet, efficient demeanor had somehow given Broadstreet pause today. Consequently, he hadn't found any cracks in her testimony, even if he had been making none-too-subtle insinuations about Cassidy and Professor Randall Greene, who'd gotten fired in a most public manner under suspicious circumstances. To add to Broadstreet's failure, Cassidy had firmly shut down the president when he'd hinted about her "personal troubles," as well.

That's right. Instead of allowing her inquisitor to rile her up, Cassidy had maneuvered the conversation toward Gilbert's accomplishments, refusing to allow Broadstreet any leeway in his questioning, hinting about the president's own reasons for holding this trial.

Thus, Gilbert had finally come out a winner.

Cassidy locked gazes with Rachel, then walked over to her. "Broadstreet's not infallible. Just remember— robot underwear."

Gilbert's eyebrow shot up. "I don't know what robots have to do with anything, but I know Rachel's not going to let me down. Isn't that so?"

A spark of hope flickered inside of her.

Yes, she thought, *I'm going to tear Broadstreet to shreds. And I can do it without having to reveal any of Gilbert's secrets.*

A welcome voice interrupted her musings. "You ready to chew some bubble gum and kick ass?"

Ian.

She whirled around to find him standing there, holding a large brown bag and wearing a confident grin. Rachel didn't know why, but suddenly she felt infused, pumped up and indestructible.

With a jerk of his chin, Ian invited her to follow him, and she did. He led her out of the noisy room and down the hall, where they halted at a spot near an out-of-the-way closet marked Supplies and a water fountain.

Once there, he took some food—chips, two peanut butter and jelly sandwiches and soda—out of the bag. "Join me?"

It looked as if he'd stopped by the campus store earlier, and his consideration touched her.

"You knew I'd be too flighty to fill my stomach, huh?" she asked.

"Maybe 'excited' is a better description for how you're probably feeling."

As they broke into their lunch, she flashed him a grateful smile. He took care of her, this guy, and she couldn't figure out a good-enough reason for him to do so.

Well, actually, she probably could, if she looked deep enough into the blue of his eyes.

But she couldn't. Not now. Not until later, when today was behind her.

"I read your article this morning," she said. "It was great. You were right about the students and their support of Gilbert. I'm happy they're speaking up."

"Yeah." He nodded and leaned against the wall. "Me, too. My editor wasn't thrilled about the lack of…what did he say?…oh, yeah…*interesting angles,* but I think I got the job done. We've been getting positive public feedback also, so life's lookin' good."

"It is." She took a swig of her soda, thinking she hadn't tasted something so wonderful in years. "It really is."

She finished the first half of her sandwich, scooping a few chips into her mouth from the bag he was holding.

This was intimate, she realized, sharing lunch like this, her hand nudging his as she dug into the bag. It was also comfortable, knowing she didn't need to talk to fill the silences.

They ate in companionable peace for a few minutes, and she rested her body against the wall, too, echoing his posture.

"I owe you a meal or two, you know," she said.

"You don't owe me a thing."

Oh, she begged to differ. Last night at the bookstore, she'd chickened out once again while trying to tell someone about the documents. She'd started to mention them only to stop herself, to leave Ian without giving him what she'd promised.

A decent interview.

Ian finished his meal and crumpled up the wrappings. "I would, however, like to see you for a follow-up after your testimonial."

"You've got it." Because Rachel was going to not only survive Broadstreet this afternoon—she was going to come out the winner.

Damn straight she was.

"And then," she added, "maybe I can have you over to my place. I'm not a great cook, but I'll do my best for you."

"I'll bet you can whip up a storm in the kitchen."

She thought of her adoptive parents and how they'd criticized her culinary efforts time and again. "Seriously, Ian, I don't play Martha Stewart all that much. But I can make edible spaghetti."

"Did I ever tell you how much I love spaghetti?"

As a sassy answer, she wadded up her own wrappings, then took Ian's trash also, stuffing everything in the big bag. With a saucy glance, she walked to the nearest garbage container and threw everything away.

He watched her the entire time, his gaze going from

assessing to smoky, piercing blue to a foggy mist of mountain haze. She could almost see what was going through his mind—the same thing that was going through hers.

Sultry images that made her dizzy.

Meeting his eyes, she sauntered over to him, taking her time because he seemed to like the way she was moving. Taking her time because she wasn't quite sure what she was going to do when she arrived in front of him.

When he spoke, his voice was low, a little ragged. "All I want to do right now is kiss you, Rachel."

Lightning burned through her, introducing the slow thunder of arousal under her skin.

"Are you trying to distract me?" she asked, surprised at how playful she sounded.

"No." He ran a longing glance down her body, then up again. "I'm just remembering what happened between us the other day, when I kissed you and you seemed to like it."

She was inches from him now, a stuttering heartbeat away.

"I did," she said. "I liked it a lot."

Too much. But...

In the next breath, she was on her tiptoes, hands braced against his strong chest, sliding her body against his as she angled her chin upward for that kiss.

Yet, for a maddening second, he only held her face in his hands, pausing.

"Ian," she said, half plea, half command.

He rubbed his thumbs over the hollows of her cheeks, thrilling her right down to her toes. The hunger in his gaze only added to her impatience.

But then, with a rush of heat, she took charge, taking his lower lip into her mouth, sucking and toying with him until his grip tightened around her. Groaning, he deepened the kiss, traveling one hand up her spine, burying the other into the kinky hair that had driven her batty for most of her life.

But he seemed to enjoy the thickness of it, and that made her love it, too. His fingers massaged her scalp, as if he wanted to explore a luxury she'd never appreciated before.

Melting into him, Rachel gave in, forgetting all her doubts about why he was attracted to her, forgetting that she didn't belong anywhere...

...or to anyone.

Because, right now, she did belong. She fit right against him, just as if God had created half a circle and her curves connected Ian fully. Wonderfully.

Perfectly.

As he drew back and looked at her, caressing her cheek, her chin, her neck, Rachel's breath hitched, never having experienced the intensity of the emotion that weighed his gaze now.

Never feeling as powerful as she did at this moment.

"Thank you," she said, the word barely getting past her throat.

He smiled. "For what?"

"For..." Impulsively, she gave him one last kiss, lingering against his lips as she whispered, "For that."

For a connection that built her up.

And made her feel like she owned the world.

Ian watched Rachel at the table while she lauded Gilbert in front of the board.

He couldn't restrain a surge of pride. Who knew that she would come off so well? Not only was she sweet and upbeat—two qualities that had immediately won over the audience, Ian noted—but she was confident in answering the president's introductory questions.

Sure, Ian was trying to tamp down all the feelings she'd stirred up during the break, because that's what a reporter should do—take unbiased stock of a situation and be fair in the telling.

But how could he distance himself now?

Ian was more involved with his subject than he'd like to admit, and that pricked at him.

He'd *definitely* lost his edge.

Still, he wasn't regretting it. No way. He was a seasoned professional who could do his job no matter the circumstances, and he would do just that, dammit.

In spite of any attraction blazing between them.

As Rachel kept charming her way through her testimonial, Ian thought she had it in the bag, just like Cassidy during her own time in front of the board.

But then it happened.

President Broadstreet was smiling at Rachel's latest

comment. Yet the tight gesture struck Ian as false, and it raised his hackles.

Broadstreet had something up his sleeve, didn't he?

This was anything but a surprise, since Cassidy Maxwell had gotten the better of him earlier. But Rachel could handle it. Ian was as sure about that as the day was long.

"Now we come to the part," the president said, "where my confusion takes over, Ms. James. You see, I've paid very careful attention to your records."

Ian paused in his note-taking, recalling what Rachel had told him last night. Bad grades. Financial aid.

Could this have anything to do with the mysterious benefactor who had been helping everyone else in her group, too?

At Broadstreet's comment, Rachel had flinched ever so slightly, as if the president had reached over and pinched her. Yet she still kept her wits about her.

Don't lose it, Rachel, Ian thought. *You can run circles around him.*

"It seems," Broadstreet continued, "that you had quite a financial-aid package, Ms. James. Far beyond what most students have access to at Saunders. And I'm also wondering about these grades…. Like your friend David Westport, your grades don't reflect the type of student this university welcomes."

Bastard.

Again, Rachel's interview rang in Ian's ears. *My adoptive parents sometimes told me I was dumb….*

While she recovered from Broadstreet's low blow, Gilbert looked on. The professor seemed ready to jump out of his chair to defend her.

Ian paid closer attention. It wasn't that Gilbert hadn't been concerned about his other students, but there was something off here. The otherwise easygoing professor was showing a little more anger than he'd exhibited during previous testimonials, a little more panic.

Rachel was his favorite student, Ian reminded himself. And he's not hiding it.

So why was Gilbert's reaction niggling at him?

"I was surprised by Saunders' response, as well," Rachel said calmly. "But I figured they wanted *me* to fulfill an affirmative-action quota."

"Not quite." Broadstreet lavished a superior smile on her. "Saunders attracts brilliant scholars of every race, color and creed. We don't need to reach for students with grades like yours."

Ian's spine stiffened. Next to him, Joe even noticed his agitation. The photographer pulled on Ian's sweater, as if tugging on a pit bull's chain.

This time, Gilbert sat up in his chair and pointed a finger at Broadstreet, no longer the complacent observer. "Your rudeness is out of line."

"I'm telling it like it is, Mr. Harrison." Broadstreet held up his hands in an ingenuous shrug. "That's why we're here, isn't it?"

"Excuse me," Rachel asked. "Is this going anywhere?"

Ian mentally cheered her tenacity. Even if she was starting to seem vulnerable, she was still hanging in there.

"I see," Broadstreet said, "that we need to get to the point here. Ms. James, how did you come to receive such a grand financial-aid package? It's strange that you had turned down Saunders' invitation to attend, and only *then* the package was offered. It's almost as if you were being lured here." The president smirked.

"I—"

Rachel stopped, obviously at a loss as to how to continue.

"You didn't expect that financial-aid package at that point, did you, Ms. James?"

Rachel didn't say a word, staring at the table in obvious frustration instead.

"Would it be out of the question," Broadstreet continued, "to say that you also were the recipient of a gift, a present from that anonymous benefactor we've heard so much about?"

She was shaking her head, clearly torn about what she was going to say. Once, Ian had put her in the exact same spot, asking her about this benefactor. She hadn't answered him then, but he had wondered how much she knew.

"I repeat," Broadstreet added, getting out of his chair and stalking toward Rachel. "Why would someone in the financial-aid office take the time to put together such an extensive package if you hadn't committed to

Saunders? Why were they courting a below-average student, Ms. James?"

Even from this distance, Ian could see the tears in Rachel's eyes. He couldn't help taking a step forward, but once again, he was stopped by Joe.

And the own jerk of his conscience.

Reporters do not interfere, he told himself. Do your job.

Broadstreet stood next to Rachel's chair, waving his papers at her. "Why, Ms. James?" He bent even lower, next to her face. "Why?"

"I don't know!" she ground out, jaw clenched, voice breaking.

Gilbert sprang out of his chair, inserting himself between Rachel and Broadstreet. "Leave her *alone*."

"Why, Gilbert?"

Broadstreet tossed his papers on the table, and Rachel put a hand over her eyes, showing Ian and the entire room that she'd failed. His heart cracked wide open, bleeding for her.

For a sublime few moments, she'd seemed so proud of herself, but now that was crushed.

Seething, the professor hesitated to answer Broadstreet.

With a disgusted sneer, the president turned his attention back to Rachel, starting to fire another question at her, but Gilbert stopped him. In fact, he stole all the oxygen out of the room with what he said.

"I'm the one who offered her the financial-aid package."

Silence.

"Gilbert," Rachel finally said, reaching up to grab his tweed jacket, "don't."

He ignored her, his gaze targeted on Broadstreet.

"I'm your mysterious benefactor, Alex. Now, leave her alone."

As the president's mouth widened in a victorious smile, Rachel shot a horrified glance to her friends, who were sitting stone-still in their seats, along with the rest of the stunned audience.

Ian had his story, all right.

Why had he admitted it? Rachel thought, her sight swimming as Gilbert and Broadstreet faced off.

This was her fault. If she'd been able to hold the president off as effectively as Cassidy had done, Gilbert wouldn't have had to come to the rescue.

Again.

What had he just sacrificed for her? Would the breaking of his silence have worse consequences?

Broadstreet answered only a fraction of her questions as he addressed the board and then the audience. "So, we have in our midst a man of good deeds. It's only too bad that he broke myriad rules to see his charity through. Am I right, Mr. Harrison? Grade tampering, playing God with the lives of the students and heaven knows what else? How can you possibly justify all this?"

"Alex," Gilbert answered, a man resigned to his fate, "if you have to ask, then you won't understand."

"Ah, yes. A martyr. I'm sure many in this room can understand your philanthropic attitude, but you've made a mockery of our system. It also makes me wonder what *else* you've lied to the board about. I shudder to hazard any guesses."

As Broadstreet strode away, cock of the walk, Rachel sought Gilbert's gaze. When she found it, he seemed deflated, as if the life had been sucked out of him.

And it was because of her.

She'd been a disappointment to him once more because, instead of being able to save him with her testimonial, she'd brought him down.

Before she fully retreated into herself, she saw that Ian was watching her carefully, compassionately, and it wrenched her apart because she couldn't stand the pity.

Dammit, she'd been the victim too many times before, and she was tired of it.

It was time to do something for Gilbert now, even if he had so many things to answer for.

"Mr. Broadstreet," she said, "think of what Gilbert's done—and is doing—for so many students, kids who can't find their way through a very muddled time in their lives. That counts for a lot."

The president froze in his steps, then pivoted to face her. "It's too bad you didn't finish your education, Ms. James, because you might have learned an appreciation for how the world works. There are rules and a certain order. It's not up to people like Gilbert Harrison to fly in the face of the establishment, to pervert what makes this institution run so well. So, in answer, certainly, Gilbert's kind soul does count for something, but he's lied to us for years. He manipulated our trust in a truly devious manner. We do not operate that way, Ms. James. Surely even you can understand that."

And…case closed.

Before she could tell him to go to hell, before Gilbert could even speak up and before all her friends raised their voices, cameras began flashing.

Broadstreet took the microphone to amplify his voice. "I see no need to entertain more character witnesses because the board already has heard a plethora of them. Mr. Harrison has had ample opportunity to defend himself and we'll take the testimonials into consideration while we decide if this faculty member will remain with Saunders or be terminated. Thank you."

With that, he shot out of the room, flanked by the rest of the board. The audience went wild, shouting at Broadstreet as Ian, of all people, bolted from his side of the room over to Gilbert, ushering him out of the hall and through a back door.

His decisive reaction wasn't lost on Rachel. In fact, it bathed her in such overwhelming gratefulness that a sob racked her body.

He'd been able to save Gilbert, even in a small way.

And that was more than she could say for herself.

Chapter Eight

Straightaway, Ian Beck had made sure that Gilbert was spirited off and kept away from any overzealous community members and journalists.

At least, that was what the reporter had told him, and Gilbert didn't have the energy to question his motives.

He was about to get fired, wasn't he? And nothing else mattered right now.

As Gilbert sat on Ian's hotel room sofa, he felt the last of his preciously held zest drain out of him. Thirty-one years of educating young people, helping them for the better, watching them grow up to become successful and to make the world a better place. He loved every one of those kids, and they had gifted him with such wonderful purpose in return.

Teaching had been his dream. So how had all of this become such a nightmare?

Ian brought him a mug of coffee, dark and strong. The reporter looked genuinely concerned, and Gilbert barely had the sense to wonder why that was.

"Thank you for taking me out of there," Gilbert said, merely holding the coffee mug. He was almost too numb to feel the warmth of it against his palms, or to suspect if the reporter would begin asking questions.

"No problem, Professor. I've already called Rachel to let her know where you are. She's getting the gang together and they'll be here in a minute."

Earlier, Ian had explained that he was bringing Gilbert to the Paul Revere Hotel just off campus because it was the nearest and most private place he could think of to shelter the professor. Gilbert hadn't complained. He had barely even been aware of what was happening.

"Is there anything I can do for you?" Ian asked.

Gilbert attempted a smile, but failed. "There's nothing anyone can do now."

The reporter's gaze sharpened, as if his mind was whirring with ideas to the contrary. "I don't know about that. Maybe—"

He was interrupted by a knock on the door.

"Hold that thought," Ian said, moving to the peephole.

He glanced out of it, then opened up. Gilbert's group of ex-students swarmed into the room, rushing up to him, all of them asking how he was faring.

Ella Gardner got to Gilbert first, and the look of pure relief on her face threw him into grief. She'd been the initial guardian of his benefactor secret. He'd put her through so much.

And for what? Where had discretion gotten him?

As she hugged Gilbert, trying to comfort him, he saw that the others felt the same way she did. Why weren't they more shocked at his revelation?

"Did all of you know?" he asked.

Ella seemed tentative. "I was conflicted about keeping your secret, Gilbert, so I told the group. I was convinced you had nothing to hide, especially in light of what was happening with Broadstreet. But we all decided to respect your wishes and not give you even more to worry about, to keep your secret unless the worst happened. After Cassidy gave her testimonial, we thought revealing it wouldn't be necessary, but you ended up letting the cat out of the bag, anyway."

He should have felt betrayed, but he couldn't. Instead, he was ashamed, indebted to these people who still stood by him.

Besides, none of it was going to make a difference now.

"I'm only sorry your pains came to naught," he said.

As they assured him it was okay, they took up seats around the room, which besides being furnished with a king-size bed, also held a kitchenette and a large desk that boasted Ian Beck's computer and work materials. Some of the men remained standing. The space didn't offer enough places for everyone to sit.

Although Gilbert was finally able to look each of his friends in the eye, he was having a harder time with Rachel. She hung near the back of the room, clearly avoiding him. Was it because she believed that she had been his downfall?

Gilbert's heart softened. Her anguish was also his very own. Good Lord, he wished he could tell her that. What if she knew that he had put together that financial-aid package for the very reason of bringing her to Saunders? Alex Broadstreet hadn't been far off the mark when he had suggested a similar scenario.

The president just hadn't known the specifics, thank goodness. He hadn't known of the joy Gilbert had felt when he had first seen Rachel's application.

Gilbert realized that everyone was watching him, waiting for him to say something. In the back of the room, he saw Ian Beck whispering to Rachel. Then the reporter opened the door and snuck out.

Odd. Considering the way Ian had saved Gilbert from the crowds, wouldn't a journalist also try to convince everyone to allow him to stay so he could get his story?

Gilbert cleared his throat. "I'm sorry it turned out this way."

Nate Williams was the first to speak up. His hair was rumpled, as if he had been running his fingers through it. "This whole hearing was a joke, Gilbert. I'm going to make sure Broadstreet pays. He ignored the established guidelines for Saunders conduct board hearings."

Ella, a federal prosecutor, backed him up on that.

Chuffing, Jacob Weber said, "Did anyone else find the irony in how he was breaking the rules while accusing Gilbert of doing the same?"

They were only trying to make him feel better, because they knew just as well as Gilbert did that he was about to get fired and lose one of the only reasons he had to get up in the mornings anymore.

Jane Jackson, his administrative assistant, had taken a seat next to Gilbert on the sofa, resting a hand on his arm. "Gilbert, everyone knows that Broadstreet's been on your back for years. I swear, the guy is jealous of you. All the affection you get from the students, all the respect you've earned from the staff—Broadstreet's had none of it. I think he was unpopular in high school and he's taking his revenge out on the homecoming king, if you know what I mean."

"What comes around goes around," David Westport said. "He'll get his due."

The room fell into awkward silence. All of them were waiting for Gilbert to explain, of course.

Why had he kept such a secret when all he had ever wanted to do was good? they were wondering. And what else was he not talking about?

From her spot in the corner, Rachel watched him with that bruised gaze. He owed her the most explanations, but he couldn't say a word. Maybe not ever.

"I'm sure you've pieced my reasoning together," he said. The coffee had grown cold in his hands, so he set the mug on an end table. "But here's the truth, right from the beginning."

Rachel leaned against the wall, pulling her coat around her body.

And I wish I could tell you more, he thought.

"At one time in each of your academic careers," he said, "you came upon some trouble, whether it was personal, emotional, financial or academic. Even though your situations differed, you had one thing in common—all of your difficulties threatened to ruin your goals and ambitions, or maybe they even threatened your lives. At that point, whether you knew it or not, you received aid from an anonymous benefactor—something tailored to your situation. The only stipulation was that you would be expected to repay this favor someday. And you did by showing up here for me, offering testimonials to save my job." He managed a tight laugh. "Which you almost did."

"But it didn't work out that way," Smith Parker said, standing next to Jane.

"We tried our damnedest, though, didn't we?" Gilbert asked, not wanting them to suffer, too. "And you were at an unfair advantage, because I couldn't reveal that I was the benefactor."

"Why?" asked Eric Barnes.

Gilbert hesitated, knowing he needed to finally break a promise he had kept for years. "My grandfather had won some money just before he passed away, and I inherited everything. I was his favorite."

He couldn't help glancing at Rachel, who was watching the floor, hands stuffed in the pockets of that coat, one that desperately needed replacing. He longed to buy her a new one, not only because he wanted her to shine but because he still felt protective—even if all he could do was keep her from being cold or feeling inferior.

But he wouldn't think about that now. The truth might creep into his explanation or show on his face.

Gilbert continued, restraining himself. "I had to promise never to reveal the inheritance because my grandfather had feared the family might go at one anothers' throats. I kept my word for as long as I could, using some of the money to pay for my schooling so that I could stay in the world of academia and support my family at the same time. And I needed every penny. You know what they pay teachers, don't you?"

A few of the ex-students laughed, and Gilbert's spirits lifted, just as they always did around the young.

"The salary is next to nothing," Gilbert added. "At the same time, I wanted to continue my grandfather's philanthropy, so I decided to help others, too. I thought I could go on that way forever, but that wasn't the case. There's always someone who ruins what's good and right. This time, it was Alex Broadstreet."

"He'll get his," Nate repeated.

"It doesn't matter anymore." Gilbert sighed, thinking of all the positive changes he could have continued if Broadstreet hadn't decided to step in. Bitterness threatened to overcome him, but he fought it, pushing it away and hiding from the negativity.

But with one look at Rachel, he realized something: the two of them handled their problems in the same manner—by withdrawing.

Rosemary, he thought, conjuring the name of another woman he had wanted to help so badly, the woman who had needed more from him than he was able to give. *I'm so sorry. I failed your daughter when all I wanted to do was help her attain the life she deserves.*

Moisture stung the corner of his eye. Jane must have sensed his utter helplessness because she hugged him.

"You only meant the best, Gilbert," she said. "We're here to help you work things out, okay?"

Everyone supported her on that, standing and coming to him.

Even Rachel, who wiped away her own tears and finally walked out of her corner. He stood, meeting her, wrapping her in his arms and holding her tight as she cried against him.

"I let you down," she whispered.

"Shh," he said. "That's not true, Rachel. Not true at all."

They stayed like that for a moment, sharing strength, until his phone rang. Everyone froze.

Ring.

Ring.

Feeling like he was inspecting a jail cell where he

would be spending his life sentence, Gilbert checked the incoming number.

It was Alex Broadstreet.

When Ian returned, he found Rachel waiting for him, sipping tea on the couch in the otherwise empty hotel room.

She'd called five minutes before, letting him know that everyone was getting ready for the hearing's decision, which would be read in two hours, thus giving the press enough time to gather again. But he was stunned when she told him that she didn't want to go with the rest of the gang for the rendering.

"I'd rather wait for you," she'd said, getting him right *there*, in the heart.

And he wanted to be with her, too, because Ian suspected that this would be a very public bloodbath. A decision this speedy didn't bode well for Gilbert, especially with Broadstreet at the helm.

Shutting the door behind him, Ian doffed his jacket, tossed it on the bed and walked toward her. He'd consumed a beer or two in the hotel bar, thus helping him to justify his decision to rescue Gilbert, only to leave the room without an exclusive story.

The reporter in him wondered what the hell he'd been thinking. There'd been a scoop right in his own room and he'd turned his back on it, giving in to some inner cry for decency.

Leaving the group alone had seemed right, humane.

Sticking around and snooping would've only throttled a conversation that the gang needed to have—and it would've been a slap in Rachel's face.

He cared too much about her to do that.

As a result, she'd thanked him over the phone for his thoughtfulness, and as much as Ian hated to admit it, her gratitude was worth more than this story he was supposed to be pursuing come hell or high water.

Now Rachel's hands were shaking as she drank the tea. But she soon gave up, positioning the cup on the end table next to Gilbert's abandoned coffee. While doing so, she spilled some onto her coat, which was draped over the arm of the sofa.

"Damn." She swiped at the wet stain, her voice thick, as if she was about to cry.

Without a word, Ian went into the bathroom and came out with a cup of water and some tissues. He wasn't sure what else to do.

Neither was Rachel, obviously. She accepted the items from him with a tremulous smile, then scrubbed.

"What time are you all meeting tonight?" he asked.

"Eight o'clock."

From her phone call, he knew that she'd invited her friends over to her place. Maybe she was doing it as an apology, since she felt she'd failed everyone. At any rate, she'd explained that, wherever they ended up, they would be either celebrating or commiserating with one another, anyway. It might as well happen at her home.

She gave up wiping at the spot, abandoning the tissues along with her tea. "You're invited, too, Ian. We all wanted to get together tonight as friends, not as an official Gilbert posse. But if you're lucky, maybe Gilbert will agree to talk to you about his benefactor story or…I don't know. Maybe it's too soon or just altogether inappropriate. I shouldn't make those kinds of promises."

It was on the tip of his tongue to refuse her invitation, even with the possibility of obtaining the exclusive benefactor information, but he really didn't want to. His assignment was ending, and every last minute he could get with this woman was precious.

Damn, he was going to miss Rachel.

He sat next to her on the sofa. God, he could smell that jasmine floating off of her skin. He imagined her dabbing it behind her ears, in the dip between her collarbones.

"I'll be there," he said.

At least until he had to leave.

Clearly cheered by his words, she turned toward him, drawing her legs up on the cushions so her skirt covered them. She had taken off her boots, and the tips of her stockings peeked out. It was all Ian could do not to reach for a toe, teasingly tweak it, reestablishing the easy connection he'd enjoyed with her earlier today.

Why did being around her take him to a higher level of contentment? And was it too much to hope that she felt the same way?

It sure looked like she did, with both of them sitting here like this, smiling at each other, lifting each other up.

"I'm glad you're coming," she said. "Things aren't going to be the same after you're gone."

As Ian realized just how strongly he was starting to feel about her, he wanted to turn tail and leave. Yeah, just *leave,* for God's sake. But, then again...

He didn't want to go anywhere.

He was happy being right here, smelling her perfume, talking just *this* much louder than a whisper, flirting with the edge of that cliff he was thinking about jumping over.

He decided to lay it on the line, just as he'd done this afternoon when he'd admitted that he wanted to kiss her again. "I'm going to miss you, Rachel."

She smiled softly, wonderingly. "Really? I mean..."

"Why would you be surprised at that? You know I'm attracted to you."

Absently, she licked her lips, drawing Ian's attention to them. Heat flooded his belly, the sensation throbbing outward, downward, reminding him of just how much he'd been dreaming about her.

Red suffused her face, darkening her skin. "It's... been a long time for me. You know. Playing these games, being alone in a room with a guy I'm attracted to also."

The admission must've been hard for her, because she immediately glanced away and started spinning a lock of hair around her finger. But she stopped fidgeting immediately, as if she was chiding herself for getting nervous.

"I'm glad we're getting all this out in the open," he said, reaching for the strand she had abandoned, twirling it around his own finger. He loved her hair, the wildness and complexity of it.

She seemed to enjoy his attentions, leaning into his hand as he ran his fingers into more of her curls, massaging and soothing her.

"You have no problems with…" She hesitated, motioned to herself and then to him.

"What?"

She pointed to her skin.

"Our races?" He grinned. "I've seen a lot of the world, Rachel, and believe me, I've experienced things that make it necessary to look past a person's surface and under all the trappings. Everyone is born, everyone copes with love, everyone dies. The details differ, but it's all about the souls. That's what makes a person."

She was watching him as if he was so wise, so valuable. He accepted it, treasuring the way she perceived him.

"Even after all these years," she said, "I'm afraid of what people might say if they saw us walking down the street together. I can't deal with them staring, judging."

"Boston's the last place you'd have to worry about that." He slipped his hand downward, so that his thumb stroked her throat.

She made a contented sound. "I'm talking in generalities."

How much intolerance had she fought during her life? He could only guess, based on what she'd told him about growing up.

"Ian?"

Carefully, he rested the other hand on her knee, rubbing her, testing her. "Yeah?"

"So tell me. Are you full of hot air or have you been with a woman like me?"

He didn't want to go into what he was full of right now. But whatever it was, it was set to explode into sparks.

"I don't want to think about anyone else, Rachel."

A beat passed as she bit her lip.

She was fighting herself, Ian thought, but why? Were there even more reasons?

As he wondered how to handle this, she leaned forward, kissing him with all the passion he'd imagined she possessed. She consumed him, took him over, his body flaring with the fire of his hunger for her.

Pushed as far as he could go, he pressed her closer to him: lips against lips, chest against chest. He devoured her as he had during all those nighttime fantasies, where he'd wake up in a sweat and never get back to sleep.

When she shifted backward, pulling him down with her to the sofa pillows, he followed, running his mouth down her chin, her neck, nipping at the warm, tender spot below her ear and making her wince and squirm beneath him.

He traveled a hand under her sweater, over the silk of her belly, her rib cage, skimming over a small, firm breast. Sliding the lace of her bra cup downward, he stroked his fingertips over a nipple. It puckered for him, hard and sensitive.

"Mmm." Feverishly, Rachel guided his other hand under the wool, forcing the material up, inviting him to go further.

Never one to waste an opportunity, he nuzzled aside her sweater and eased down the bra with both hands so that both of her breasts were exposed. Gently, he licked one, circled his tongue around the aroused nub, sucking at her.

Arching upward, she encouraged him, moving her hips and holding his head to her chest.

"Ian," she said with a sigh, "you feel so good...."

He ground himself against her, showing just how much he wanted her. He was hard and ready, nudging against the softness between her legs.

Going too fast, he thought. *Stop soon or...*

When she jerked his shirt out of his pants, he caught his breath, the warmth of her palms against his back too much to handle.

Dammit, he needed to slow it down or this would be over before it really started.

Taking in a deep breath, he pushed to his elbows, removing his weight from her.

Ian's groin was pounding, demanding to know why he'd stopped. But if he didn't calm himself down right now, there'd be no chance of making their first time last as long as he wanted it to.

Mind over matter, Ian thought. *She's worth more than one short romp on a couch.*

Disappointed curiosity had widened her dark eyes.

"Let's switch to a lower gear," he whispered into her ear.

His libido was never going to forgive him. Right now, his nether regions were screaming, stomping like a mob that had gone to riot. "I've been fantasizing about what it would be like with you, Rachel, and I want it to be…"

She rubbed her cheek against his. "What?"

In answer, he rose up again and kissed her, long and sweet, just to validate that he did still desire her with every throbbing inch of his body. Then he drew away.

"Slower," he said, grinning. "A ride that lasts and lasts."

Rachel laughed, panting a little, her fingers skittering from his back to his stomach, where she ran her nails up and down him with maddening promise.

"How slow?" she asked.

"Like honey during winter."

As she drew a finger down his nose, loving the shape of it, she had no doubt that he was telling the truth. He wouldn't have told her that she was unlike any other woman if he intended to dump her.

But how could she have so much trust in a man she'd only known for a short time? Was it because he'd played hero to her, then to Gilbert? She wasn't sure, yet there were some things you just *knew*.

Ian was a man to keep.

Too bad he wouldn't be staying around to make that a possibility.

But she'd thought it before and she thought it again: his fleeting presence in her life was one of his appealing qualities. She didn't expect much more of men or people in general. And when he was gone, everything she'd invested in him would disappear, too.

Including the secrets she couldn't bear to keep inside any longer.

He traced the tips of his fingers down her cheek, looking as if he was drinking in every angle, every feature. It made her feel vulnerable yet beautiful at the same time.

Was he for real about the difference in their ethnicity? She'd spent too much time worrying about it, and pushing the concern aside was tough, especially while under such close, affectionate inspection.

But she *wanted* to believe him. That was the thing.

She didn't care what anyone else thought about them being together.

"Do you think we should just neck?" she asked, letting him know that a slow drive would be fine and dandy with her.

As a matter of fact, his insistence on making this perfect thrilled her. It healed her heart.

In answer, he rested his lips against her temple. His chest rose and fell, his breathing evening out. All too easily, she fell into his pattern, the material of his sweater rough against her skin, her bared breasts.

While they paused, she merely enjoyed the feel of his weight as he rested half on top of her. The feel of a man's muscles and girth, the scent of his soap, the taste of him still in her mouth.

So good. So right.

But a few minutes later, he was back to kissing her. Necking, as she'd said.

Two first-timers exploring each other and making it last.

At least until they had to return to Saunders, a place where he would go back to being the reporter and she would go back to supporting the story—Gilbert Harrison, a man who just might have lost his career today.

Chapter Nine

The evening newscast showed the entire nightmare.

Professor Gilbert Harrison sat calmly at a table, facing President Alex Broadstreet and the board while awaiting the decision. Students and supporters gathered around their favorite teacher as flashbulbs went off.

Only the most astute observer could tell that the respondent wasn't as composed as he seemed. One of his eyes twitched at the corner, as if every part of him was holding together except for this lone chink—a defect in his armor.

"Today," the local female reporter said in a voice-over, "the hearing of a Saunders professor came to a close, thus ending a story that has caught the attention of the Boston area for its important question—can we trust the people who are educating our children?"

The screen then switched to President Broadstreet, who rendered the board's decision.

"In light of testimonials from former Saunders students," he said, all but gleaming in the spotlight, "we as a board have decided to terminate the employment of Gilbert Harrison."

The reporter's voice took over as the entire hall broke into chaos. "So in spite of the professor's evident popularity and the revelation that he was anonymously giving away thousands upon thousands of dollars to students in need, Broadstreet commented that the reputation of Saunders University would not be compromised by having a man who has, quote, 'lied his way through several dishonorable situations.' Mr. Harrison himself was not available for comment, and that leaves us to wonder—just what has been going on at Saunders?"

As the journalist signed off, the focus again captured Gilbert Harrison, who seemed frozen in his chair, his face pale, his eyes empty.

And as the camera further closed in on him, it ruthlessly showed an image that broke the hearts of many viewers that night.

In this man, they saw someone who'd lost everything.

Even as those around him embraced him.

Once at Rachel's house, they all tried to cheer up their mentor. Tried to laugh and joke and avoid the sadness that lingered over Gilbert's head like a cloud that had spent all its rain.

But he had been fired, and nothing they said could change that.

No matter what they did, Gilbert had remained seated in a corner chair all night, never touching the pot-luck food that was brought to him, staring into space instead of interacting with the people who loved him.

Ian, for his part, had been a godsend, Rachel thought now, watching him as the evening came to a close and he said goodbye to everyone at the door. He'd mingled with her friends as if they'd all known one another for years. And she could tell they liked him, too.

Heck, even Sandra and Jane had kept giving her the "okay" sign when Ian wasn't looking.

Yes, that had been the high point of the night—Ian and the interest he stirred up among her friends. He'd promised them early on that he wasn't here for a story, and Rachel had loaned her agreement, having already been convinced herself.

His kisses were too real, she thought—no, *hoped.* She couldn't imagine him betraying her.

And after about an hour of wariness, the gang had finally relaxed around him.

Still, Ian's friendliness hadn't erased Gilbert's debil-itating silence. The older man resembled someone who'd been robbed and didn't know how to start over. Frus-tratingly, not one of them could cheer him up, either, or make him realize that this wasn't the end of the world.

Now, as the gang left the gathering with Gilbert in tow, Rachel and Ian waved to them.

Odd to have him standing here next to her, she thought, just like a husband and wife in their little house.

Just like her and Isaac.

She tucked the image of her former husband back into her memories. Before he'd died, he'd told her that the last thing he wanted was for Rachel to withdraw. He'd said that he hoped she would find happiness again someday.

Of course, she'd promised that would never happen, that she would love only him. And she'd actually believed it for a long time.

While the gang either headed for the nearest subway stop or their cars, Ian put his arm around Rachel's shoulders. Out of instinct, she leaned into him, seeking warmth, enjoying the comfort of the muscles in his arms, his chest.

Attempting to concentrate on *this* man, she kept watching as Cassidy and Eric guided Gilbert to Eric's car.

"I'm glad they volunteered to take Gilbert home," Rachel said. "I was concerned about leaving him alone tonight."

Ian squeezed her closer, allowing Rachel to let go of her worries. It also helped that Eric had told her in confidence that he would sleep on Gilbert's couch, just to make everyone feel better.

"Gilbert's got an amazing backup system," Ian said. "He'll be fine."

Admiration shone through his words, and that perked Rachel up. Maybe they hadn't handled everything perfectly with Gilbert, but they'd done their best out of love.

When Ian brushed her arm with his fingertips, something washed over her…lust, affection, she wasn't exactly sure what it was…but it compelled her to turn to him, to cup his face in her hands and kiss him. The burn of his five o'clock shadow torched her skin, but that only added to her desire.

Catching a breath, he pulled back, as surprised by the force of her emotion as she was.

"What was that about?" he asked, grinning.

"You." She shut the door and backed away from him, taking his hands in hers and leading him farther inside her house. "Nate said he respected you for what you did with Gilbert today, taking him out of Lumley Hall, then leaving us alone to talk privately. And, believe me, Nate's respect is hard-earned."

"Glad to hear it. When we were talking, he told me that some of the gang is discussing ways to help Gilbert get back on his feet. I couldn't believe it when he brought up the possibility of a group interview. He wants the community to know everyone's opinions about Gilbert's heroic side."

Nate had approached her with the idea, too, and she liked it. "Well, you're the man for the job."

They both smiled, the house quiet with just the two of them there.

A question was hanging in the air, coupled with the keen realization that they were alone together.

How long was he going to stay tonight?

It didn't take a lot of soul searching for Rachel to admit that she wanted him here for many, many more hours. This afternoon had flipped on a dangerous switch inside of her, had made her yearn for him as if he were the sustenance she'd been denied for years.

She felt so full, so contented around him.

Almost shyly, she guided him toward the couch, with its exhausted plaid upholstery and mismatched overstuffed pillows.

"Why don't you take a load off while I clean up?" she asked, thinking it was a nice start.

Yup, ease into asking him to stay, she thought.

She couldn't come right out with it. First of all, she wasn't used to acting so obvious. She was sorely out of practice with this kind of thing. Second of all, some dumb part of her conscience was afraid of his possible rejection, even though he'd shown quite a bit of interest already.

Yeah, *interest*, she thought, kidding herself. This afternoon had been a little more than *interest*.

He'd started to pull her toward the kitchen. "How about I help you clean up so you can kick back that much sooner? It's been a long day…a long week…for you."

Once again, his thoughtfulness swallowed her in giddy warmth. Did he seem like such a good man because he really was? Or did he seem like the perfect catch because he'd be leaving soon?

Or was it a bit of both?

"Seriously," she said, tugging him back toward the couch. "I want you to relax."

"Don't look a gift horse in the mouth, Rachel. Besides, the sooner you're all mine, the sooner I'll be happy."

She felt her skin go flushed. "You are *so* straightforward."

"Sorry."

"No. I like that about you. I like it a lot."

As they both just stood there, the moment expanded, ballooning with possibilities, coming close to exploding.

I like you *a lot,* she thought. *A whole, whole lot.*

But… She sighed. Things seemed to be moving so quickly between them. He scrambled her mind and that couldn't be healthy.

Knowing better than to rush into things, Rachel grinned and walked to the kitchen, leaving him standing there alone.

When he laughed in what had to be disappointment, she regretted her choice immediately, knowing that she'd gone down the wrong road. What was with her, anyway? Didn't she have it in her anymore to be with a man? And how could she allow her usual MO— avoidance—to take over?

A voice from the peanut gallery of her mind whispered, *Because you know he'll be gone soon. If you give into Ian Beck now, it'll hurt that much more when he leaves.*

And you know how much it kills you when somebody leaves.

Rachel folded her arms in front of her chest. Yes, she knew. Her natural parents. Isaac.

Being abandoned cut her apart.

"So," she said, desperate to reclaim their easy interaction, ignoring her own turmoil, "rest easy while I put everything away. I don't want all this food to spoil."

"Yes, ma'am."

He was measuring her with that piercing gaze, and she was sure that he wasn't a bit fooled by her fancyfooting around like this. Ian was too smart for that.

Nonetheless, buying herself some time, she went about wrapping up the snacks her friends had left—chips and dip, baked beans, hors d'oeuvres of every shape and color—while scolding herself.

Snap out of it, Rachel. Forget Gilbert, forget your worries, and have a little fun.

In the meantime, Ian had made his way over to the TV cabinets, where Rachel kept old videos and DVDs. He slid *Enter the Dragon* out of its slot.

"Why, Rachel James, this is unexpected."

"Oh." She held the last foil-wrapped bunch of snacks in her hands, hesitating. "Those belonged to Isaac."

Ian stared at the box, then started to put it back. "Sorry. I—"

"No, don't be sorry." And she meant it. Curiously, she was enjoying the fact that Ian had pepped up over one of Isaac's favorite movies. Her former husband might've even liked Ian, gotten along with him.

"Weird," she said. "Over the years, I've cleaned Isaac's possessions out of the closets. I gave them away to charity, but for some reason, I never got around to his flicks."

"Do you like to watch them, too?"

She nodded, then put the food in the refrigerator. "I haven't cozied up with any lately but, yeah. I did like them."

Ian seemed as if he didn't know whether or not to put the video away or to pop it into the VCR.

"It's okay," she said, running water and dish soap over a wash rag. "You can start it up if you want."

For a second, Ian's gaze sparkled like a kid on his birthday, but then he laughed, putting the box aside. "Maybe later, huh?"

Later. The word tumbled through her. What would come between now and later? More kisses and conversation? Or…?

She exhaled, calming herself and taking the wash rag to the counters, cleaning them with a vengeance. When Ian joined her in the kitchen, her skin broke out in goose bumps, prickled by his nearness.

"What was he like?" Ian asked. "Isaac?"

Rachel stopped mid-swipe, but then started up again. She'd been expecting a slap of anguish to hit her, but it hadn't come. God knew she would always hold Isaac's memory fondly. Yet wasn't this a betrayal of her dead husband? Having Ian in their house, in their kitchen?

No. Actually, Isaac might've been more distraught by Rachel's self-imposed isolation, not Ian's presence. He would've been frustrated with the way she'd closed herself off for five years. He might've even told her to get a move on already, because seeing her so alienated would have been the worst betrayal to him.

Live a little, baby, he always used to say.

And she should.

"Isaac," she said, "was a buddy to everyone. His construction crew adored him. Well, everyone adored him, as a matter of fact." Except Gilbert, but that was another story. "He was easygoing and laughed a lot. Loved food and sweets. He was older than I was— forty-three—but he had a real young soul."

"I can't imagine losing someone so vital."

"His death snuck up on us." But the financial damage hadn't. They'd been in debt long before Isaac had fallen to cardiovascular disease: his diet hadn't helped. But Rachel had loved him nevertheless, blinded by the thought that he would always be around to care for her, and she for him.

"He was lucky to have you," Ian said, "even for a short time."

Ian's compassionate tone was like a soft blanket laid

over her sadness, covering it, putting it to rest. Isaac would always be with her, and he was acknowledging that.

Rachel smiled at Ian and cleaned the wash rag. After drying her hands, she walked over to him, twining her fingers with his, skimming her thumbs over his own.

Again, the sight of his white skin against her darker shade struck her—but not as emphatically as before. In her view, they almost blended together now.

Ian followed the direction of her gaze, seeming to interpret it. "We compliment each other."

"We do." She took a step closer, reveling in the vibration of anticipation between them.

"You know," she said, "you're good for my soul."

As his eyes lit up, a pause racked the space between them. It was fraught with images of what tonight could hold: skin sliding over skin, slick kisses all over his body.

Rachel wanted to fan herself, not only because it'd gotten steamy in here, but because her drama-queen ego couldn't contain itself.

Yet, instead, she raised his hands to her mouth, pressed her lips to his knuckles, her voice muted against him. "Thank you for coming here."

"Where else would I be?"

She laughed, holding his hands under her chin, rubbing against him.

"You finished your article for tomorrow's paper?" she asked. "You don't have any more work tonight?"

The moment his fingers tensed, Rachel wanted to take it back. All she'd been doing was leading up to the big question. But, no. She'd blown it. She'd resurrected everything that had come between them before now: Ian's job.

Smooth move, big mouth, she thought.

"My article's done," he said.

And so was the damage. Subtly, he squeezed her hands, then let go of them, busying himself by closing up a bag of chips. When he gestured to a cabinet, Rachel nodded, giving him the go to store the food there.

Nice going, Rachel.

"Just so you know," he said, opening the cabinet, "I'm using some of my previous research about the benefactor. And I'll be publishing your interview as a follow-up to tomorrow's firing story."

Ah. So maybe he was feeling some remorse about having to write the rest of the articles? Is that why he'd broken away from her?

"Sounds appropriate," she said, trying to make him feel better about what he had to do. Because she knew he would take care of Gilbert. He *wanted* to.

"I'll be honest with you, though," he said. "The story reflects the truth, Rachel. Gilbert's a hero in many ways, but some people might interpret the facts like Broadstreet did."

So. There it was. The reason for his discomfort.

She swallowed, remembering how the president had

paraded his decision to fire Gilbert in front of the press. "Are you going to make a circus out of this, too?"

"Of course not."

Ian came over to her again, leaning against the counter. Though the distance between them wasn't that far, it felt like a gulf, one Rachel couldn't span.

But she tried.

She hunkered down next to him, resting on her forearms. "Thank you for that. I know you're going to handle this like a pro. I don't doubt you."

Not anymore.

"Good." He lightly pulled on her sweater. It felt as if he were asking forgiveness for having to do his job. For having it separate them.

Heartbeat accelerating, Rachel realized that she wanted *nothing* between them. God, she'd spent so long harboring secrets that she couldn't stand it anymore.

Should she tell Ian about what was in Gilbert's safe? Could he help ease her burden without giving into the temptation of using the information for his own ends?

Yes, she told herself. *If you can't trust this man after today, then whom can you trust? He won't judge you, and—remember—he'll be gone soon, taking your worries with him.*

"How well can you keep a secret?" she asked.

One of his eyebrows winged upward. "If a person wants me to keep my trap shut, I do."

"Almost like a priest, huh?"

He grinned wickedly, reminding Rachel of what they'd shared this afternoon.

"Not really," he said. Then he smoothed a hand over her back. "Why?"

Rachel's knees went weak at his touch, at the relief of feeling him again. "Gilbert's benefactor secret? It's not the only one he's been hiding. And knowing what I know is really getting to me."

Ian straightened up, concerned. "You're carrying a lot around with you."

Do it, do it, do it, urged her conscience.

"You swear not to tell anyone?" she asked.

She'd never seen a man handle a promise more seriously. "I'll take it to my grave."

Now that the revelation was at hand, she felt it all building up in her, struggling to get out: the name "Rosemary Johnson," the tension between her and Gilbert.

And when she finally let it go, she almost collapsed with relief.

"Jane found documents in his office safe," she said, "some contained in envelopes with our names on them."

Ian guided her over to a stool, where she sat down. "Do you know what all of them were?"

"No. Nobody looked in those private envelopes, but there were ledgers with numbers, things like that."

"Probably Gilbert's notes about his benefactor activities."

Her heart was still thundering, because she was

afraid of the guesses he'd make about her own documents.

"I'm sure you're right," she said. "Most of us didn't know about the benefactor until recently, but the ledger was proof. And it should've been so obvious. The fact that he was keeping *secrets* should've been obvious. Before I quit college, there was a day when I walked into Gilbert's office unannounced and he had that safe open. He freaked out on me, Ian, and yelled at me to always knock. He'd always had an open-door policy. That wasn't like him at all. Also, he was so overly concerned about his students. Shouldn't I have guessed that something was going on?"

"How could you?"

He was tracing his fingers over her arm, but she was getting more anxious by the moment.

"I've noticed other things, too, and it makes more sense now…sort of. Gilbert's always been as supportive of me as he's been with the others, yet…"

Ian merely waited for her to come around.

Rachel shifted in her seat. "Sometimes I'd catch him watching me with this expression. Almost like a grown-up watches their kid when she's won a blue ribbon. Or sometimes he'd look like he wanted to tell me something so badly…. Maybe it was because he was my benefactor, bringing me to Saunders and trying to make my life better, and he wanted to reveal that. But he had that same expression tonight, and I still can't understand what it's all about."

"Maybe he feels paternal about all of his kids?"

"Maybe." Her blood was screaming through her by now, because she knew what her next step had to be. "Why don't you look in the top drawer by the dishwasher. There's an envelope with my name on it."

As he did, he shot her a wary glance. He must've been catching her own vibes and echoing them.

He laid it on the counter.

"Open it," she said, picturing exactly what he would see in the typewritten spaces.

Mother: Rosemary Johnson.

Father: Unknown.

"These are adoption papers," Ian said.

"My adoption papers." Rachel reached out to touch his arm, thankful to finally say it. "And I'm afraid to know exactly why it is that Gilbert had them in his possession."

Gilbert sat in his easy chair while Cassidy made up the sofa for Eric. At the moment, the younger man was changing out of his day clothes in the bathroom down the hallway.

Though Gilbert had already protested the need for his former student to stay here tonight, Cassidy had changed his mind. And how could she not? Her talent for persuasion was extraordinary, and she convinced Gilbert that Eric's presence would make them all feel better.

But that was what he had always expected of Cassidy, Gilbert thought. Excellence.

He had expected that from all of his kids.

"Humiliating," he said, "having one of you on suicide watch."

"Oh, Gilbert." Cassidy fluffed a pillow. "You know that's not why Eric's here. We just want you to know you're not alone."

"I do know that, dear." He hated this darkness that had swallowed him, hated the inertia and hopelessness.

But how was he supposed to feel? His future had disappeared, almost as if it had never existed in the first place.

When Cassidy finished, she took a seat on the blanket-swathed cushions, hands folded over her knees. "In light of what happened today, I was hoping you'd make a clean sweep of your life and divulge *everything*."

He didn't have to ask what she meant. "I wanted to tell Rachel, especially now that I know it's fruitless to keep the truth hidden, but I couldn't. I even came close to taking her aside and discussing everything with her, but then I would picture the look on her face, the questions about all the decisions I had to make."

"Rachel is an adult, Gilbert, and you owe her the truth."

He owed a lot of people, Gilbert thought. Rachel, his wife and Rosemary.

A nervous laugh escaped him, soft and self-deprecating. "Perhaps I should have revealed it all. What the hell do I have to lose anymore?"

"Enough with the pity party." Cassidy sent a glance toward the hall, where Eric would be emerging soon. "I won't involve myself further with your deception, because you could right so many wrongs. Yet it takes strength to do that. All I can do is tell you that I'll be here when you need support."

Smiling affectionately, she came over to place a chaste kiss on the top of his head. "We love you, faults and all. And I know these are hard times, but you have the power to make things easier."

"Easier?"

"Gilbert." Cassidy locked stares with him, immovable. "You could make her so happy if you told her who her parents are."

That had occurred to him many times. He had pictured Rachel's blinding smile at the realization that she was indeed wanted. But he had also imagined—and feared—her rage, her betrayed sense of being left in the dark for so long.

As Eric came into the living room in a pair of sweats and a T-shirt, Cassidy leaned over to whisper in Gilbert's ear.

"Besides, she might already suspect. Did you ever think of that?"

When she stood to her full height, there was a troubled look in her eyes, as if she knew more than she was telling him.

"What—" he started.

"Think about it, Gilbert."

And, with that, she turned around to say good-night to her boyfriend.

Leaving Gilbert in his own private hell once again.

Chapter Ten

"We'll find out why Gilbert had these in his safe," Ian said, Rachel's adoption papers in hand. "I'll get to the bottom of this if you want me to."

She had the look of a woman who'd been falling from a great height, one who was reaching for someone to help her, to catch her if she required it.

And *he* was that man.

He put the documents on the counter and went to hold her, coasting his hand under her jawline, rubbing his thumb against her cheek. She closed her eyes and leaned into his every stroke.

"Ian." Her voice was barely above a whisper. "For years, I've talked myself out of finding answers, and right now, I'm still cautious about what I might find.

Who is Rosemary Johnson? And why isn't my natural father listed?"

"A closed adoption isn't going to stop us from finding out."

As he cuddled her against his chest, it occurred to Ian that, if he chose so, this would be one hell of a story. Talk about human interest. But the mere thought of turning traitor on Rachel rattled him.

Ambition or not, he didn't have it in him to hoodwink her.

And, strangely enough, he knew she had to be thinking the same thing. Otherwise, why would a suspicious woman like Rachel James trust him with this information in the first place?

As for Ian himself, he'd developed too many feelings for her to waver in his commitment. But who was he to sit here and analyze these new emotions? Too much brainwork could take the magic out of this attraction, and as off balance as this all was to him, he knew enough to enjoy it, not chase it away.

Good God, his family was going to laugh themselves silly when he told them about Rachel. *He's finally run into that brick wall we warned him about,* they would say. *Look at him, with those stars in his eyes. Mr. Ian Beck, the ultimate bachelor. He's fallen and he can't get up.*

By this time, Rachel had wrapped one arm around his waist, her face buried in his chest. He could feel the outline of her lips, even through his sweater. Or maybe he was just imagining that he could sense the heat of them, the fantasies of what could happen tonight in a bedroom down the hall.

Excitement churned in his gut, flowing down to his groin.

Grasping for control, he cleared his throat. "Before we make a plan of attack, I need to know something. You said Jane and Smith went into Gilbert's safe for those documents."

She nodded against him, causing friction, her cheek against his sweater. Quite innocently, she slipped her hands below the material to his bare back, drawing circles with her fingertips.

Clutching her tighter against him, Ian muttered a low curse. Did he have some kind of erogenous zone on his lower back that only she could locate?

"We're pretty sure Gilbert doesn't know our documents are gone," Rachel said, looking up, a tinge of passion darkening her eyes. "Jane arranged to be the one to help Gilbert clean out his office tomorrow. She's going to explain what we did before he goes into the safe himself. We're trying not to dump all of our knowledge on him at once."

Ian could barely talk now, because her hands had glided from his back to his front, exploring his belly with tentative caresses. Blood howled through him like wind through a tunnel.

"How's Gilbert…" he began.

As she moved a little lower, his throat closed. He couldn't take this anymore.

"…going to react?" Now Rachel had a slightly naughty grin on her lips, as if she knew exactly how she was affecting him and was enjoying this sensual teasing. "We're not sure. But he needs to know."

"Rachel." Her name was just a breath, a tortured whisper.

She stopped, her fingers lingering just above his belt line. "I haven't told anyone about the adoption papers, Ian. You're the first. I couldn't imagine sharing it with anyone else."

A streak of tenderness colored him. She was putting all of her faith in him, and that was responsibility at its most dangerous. No woman had ever been around long enough for this to happen before.

But was he deserving of her trust? Could he live up to it?

When he bent down to kiss her, he found his answer. Soft, warm, fulfilling. *Yes.*

He smoothed back the cloud of hair from her face. "Your trust is an honor, Rachel. I'll handle it with the care it requires. That means I won't publish any of this."

As she bit her lip, her eyes welled up, brimming with an emotion he'd never seen from a partner.

"Thank you," she said.

"I just want you to be happy." God, it was true. That's all that seemed relevant.

"So, this isn't bothering you?" she asked. "My parents could be anyone…."

"Those are your fears talking."

She shook her head, seemingly amazed at his acceptance. She'd never really found much of it before, and the fact that he'd been the one to bring it to her humbled him, stripped him bare to the soul.

He traced his fingers over the features of her face: her forehead, her cheekbones, her jaw. It was the act of a man who was seeing her for the very first time.

"Your parentage isn't what defines you," he said. "I'm interested in Rachel James, the woman who arrowed me right through the heart when I first saw her across the campus lawn. I want *that* person, complications and all."

"And I want you, too. So badly."

She splayed her hands over his stomach, sweeping upward until her palms made contact with his nipples. He flinched, turned on like a power station raging with electricity.

Their lips met again, but this was a hungrier kiss, fed by confessions and the innocent wonder of each other. While she massaged his nipples with her thumbs, making him hard in so many places, they sipped at each other, thirsting, searching and needing.

His head was thudding now, beating in time with his groin. And as they worked his sweater from his body, he found breathing a tough thing to accomplish. He was all but clawing for oxygen, but who cared? He was cutting off his air supply, anyway, as he sought her lips again, plundering deeply, their tongues stroking each other's in a desperate rhythm.

He broke away. "Let's…" His mind was a blank.

He'd forgotten what the hell he'd been about to say.

So he laughed, resuming action, anyway, guiding her back onto the kitchen stool and insinuating his hands under her skirt. He moved up her smooth thighs, sweeping his thumbs inside of them, traveling her sleek curves as he pushed the wool upward and out of the way.

Leaning backward, Rachel arched her neck, reaching over to grip the counter, making little noises that sparked Ian to no end. Encouraged, he crept his thumbs to the apex of her legs, where a pair of satiny underwear bore witness to her desire for him. The material was already moist.

"I'm ready, too," he said in a near growl.

Parting her thighs further, he slid both thumbs under the satin, delving into her wet folds, pressing, playing with the spot he knew would drive her crazy.

Her hips followed his motions, and as they locked gazes, the room temperature sizzled up a few more degrees.

By now, she had one leg wrapped around him, the other braced on the stool. As he dipped one thumb inside of her, pressing her sensitive nub with the other, she shut her eyes, looking as if she was in pain.

But Ian knew it was a nice pain, the kind you want running through your veins twenty-four hours a day. The addictive kind.

"Ian," she moaned.

"Rachel." He grinned, loving the huskiness of her

voice, loving that he could make her say his name with such hopeful demand.

"I…" She made a frustrated noise. "Oh…"

As she tensed, he eased his hands from between her legs, holding her before she fell, scooping her into his arms while she stiffened and pressed her face against his chest. As she sucked in air, he knew she'd reached a climax.

And when she bit him lightly, he knew it'd been good for her, too.

While a bare-chested Ian carried her down the hall to the bedroom, Rachel felt as if she was being roasted over a fire, turned this way and that, her skin searing, heat eating its way to her bones, into the core of her body.

She couldn't think, couldn't process anything but the mist of sweat on Ian's flesh that dampened her cheek. Couldn't concentrate on anything but the feel of him laying her on the bed and then hovering over her in the near dark.

Moonlight filtered through her curtains, emphasizing the feral gleam in his eyes, the predator's slant to his grin as he unzipped his jeans.

She watched him, lazy as a wisp of steam curling through the air.

As she lavished a gaze on him, her heart tightened, resisting for only a moment before she forced it open. Freed, she bloomed, her emotions widening, making her feel unguarded and ecstatic all at the same time.

Ian is beautiful, she thought. Tall, broad-shouldered, blessed with a firm chest that was shiny with perspiration. His waist tapered into slim hips—the physique of a man always on the go.

Sitting up, she caught a glimpse of the wispy line of hair that disappeared into his jeans, barely existing in its light softness.

Ignoring any lingering shyness, she reached out, followed the downy trail, finally, *finally* becoming the girl she'd always desired to be—the fun-loving, what-does-the-world-hold-for-us-today Rachel.

When she rested a finger below his belly button, he grabbed her wrist, but it wasn't to keep her from exploring. She coasted lower and he groaned, grip tightening then relaxing.

Oh, she liked this. She wanted to make him as happy as he said he wanted to make her, to show him how much she'd come to care for him.

"Take them off," she said quietly.

He obliged her, shucking off the jeans to reveal long muscled legs and an erection that was just waiting to find her. Before he tossed the denim away, he dove into his pocket, bringing out a condom.

"Always prepared," he said.

No surprise. Every second they'd been together had been leading up to this, and she was glad that he was responsible, not a wham-bam-thank-you-honey who took and never gave.

As she started to remove her sweater, she paused, but

only momentarily. Uncertainty still clung to her like a perfume, an essence that was hard to wash off.

She was offering her body to him. Would he take it?

When she felt a tug that indicated he was helping her to disrobe, she expanded with joy.

This man, she thought, was all she needed to make her whole.

Soon they were both naked. She scooted back toward the headboard, resting against the propped-up pillows and quirking her finger at him.

"Come on over here," she said.

Didn't sound like her. Nope. Instead she seemed like one of those sirens, an alluring woman she'd read about in her Classic Literature course years and years ago.

And she felt like one, too, especially when Ian crawled to her, positioning himself over her body.

"You're everything I fantasized about," he said. "And every inch of you belongs to me."

"You know it," she said, laughing softly.

She glowed. Not literally, of course, but she wouldn't have been surprised if her body would've started pulsing with a light that shone from beneath her skin.

The condom was within reach on the bed, so she retrieved it, unwrapped it, sheathed him with it, her fingers traveling his length.

In fervent reaction, he kissed her, and she responded like a starved woman, pressing against him as if to devour him into every famished pore. Inspired, she rolled Ian to his back, then began to plant kisses down his body, marking every taut piece of him, claiming him just as easily as he'd claimed her.

"Hey." He urged her back up to him, dug his hands into her hair, nipped at her lips. "Later. Just let me be inside you right now."

The mere words sent her pulse winging again.

As if to punctuate his meaning, he nudged against the center of her, the tip of him prodding, asking to come in.

With slow suggestion, she opened up her legs a little, slid herself against him, slippery, drenched with the orgasm she'd enjoyed.

Tested to his limit, Ian grunted out a rough laugh, then drove her to her back, seeking entrance.

At his first slow glide into her, Rachel blew out a breath. Tight. She was really tight from years of abstinence.

Ian seemed to realize it, too, because he didn't force his way in. Instead, he finessed it, seeking more bit by bit, taking his time, just like an artist mixing paint on a palette, swirling colors together, testing the texture and shade of every combination.

Gradually, she accommodated him, churning her hips to the cadence of his mounting thrusts. Sweat slicked their bodies, the stimulated tips of her breasts caressing his chest, their bellies sliding against each other's, increasing the friction, the fire.

Pleasure, she thought. *Pain.* Sharp reds and golds like spears of flame, the colors just a hint away from imitating each other, melding into one burst of blazing heat.

Rachel reached for the headboard, anchoring herself as he pounded into her with more intensity. She welcomed every hammering blow, repeating his name, urging him on, her body rising upward, an inferno reaching into the sky.

Colors…raging fires…red and gold burning and coming together, twirling into each other, flickering, licking, vibrating, exploding….

Whoooosh.

With one shattering pulsation, she imploded, her blood like lava screeching and aching through her.

Thick and spent, floating over the ground—that's how she felt as Ian strove for his own climax.

With her heart overflowing, all she wanted to do was help him to get there, bring him to the peak, shower him with complete satisfaction.

And, when he finally achieved the summit of his own passion, he collapsed, burying his face in her neck and moaning her name.

"I'm here," she said, stroking his hair, unwilling to ever let him go. "I'm not going anywhere."

And she promised herself she wouldn't.

No matter what happened.

Outside Rachel's kitchen, the morning sun fought its way through the gray sky, peeking into the window as Ian stirred a mixture of eggs, milk, garlic, salt and pepper in a bowl. Next to him, Rachel was chopping green peppers, tomatoes, green onions and already-cooked bacon. A pile of shredded cheddar cheese waited on a plate to the side.

Earlier, they'd thrown on their clothing and made an impromptu trip to the corner market so they could cook omelets together. Lord knows, they needed to eat.

Ian's belly flip-flopped when he thought about last night. They'd definitely worked up an appetite, making love to each other for hours on end and getting very little sleep.

Not that he minded. Uh-uh. In fact, he'd never felt more refreshed, more capable of tackling the world.

Even thoughts of his job—which used to define and disappoint him so regularly—were propping him up. He saw his profession in a whole new light this morning, ripe with opportunity.

He had wanted to right the wrongs in the world with his stories. Now he knew he could do it.

Cheesy. Hell, yeah, he supposed so. But the act of him and Rachel finally coming together was also life-changing, one of those moments that puts everything into perspective and illuminates all the gray areas.

Well, *almost* all of them. In the afterglow, he and Rachel were teetering on something unspoken, the question of whether he'd be leaving town now or not.

But for all Ian was concerned, he'd found a place to stay. A nest in Rachel's arms.

As she beamed at him, he wondered if she felt the

same way. Surely she did. Last night had revealed so much about both of them. It had to have persuaded her that they were meant for each other, right?

And it didn't get any simpler than that.

But when she spoke, all the hidden nooks of responsibility suddenly got a little grayer again.

"How much work do you have today?" she asked.

He sauntered over to the stove with his bowl. "A lot. I want to write up your interview and wrap up Gilbert's story. And Nate mentioned that tonight might be ideal for a group interview, if that even happens. What's up with you today?"

"Working from home. I've been doing that a lot lately."

Picking up her plates of veggies, she stood next to him, where a skillet was waiting. They'd already fried up the bacon in it, so with just a dab more butter she began to sauté the chopped vegetables.

"You want to bring your laptop and stuff over here?" she asked, bumping him with her hip, flirting. "You can interview me as many times as you like."

"Oh, tempting. So-o-o damned tempting." He watched as she stirred the green peppers and onions. The aroma made his stomach rumble.

"I'm going back to work tomorrow," she said, "and there's a chance in the near future that I could be a full-time paralegal. Nate says we might be getting the case to end all cases, which means, I think, that he'll be defending someone who really is innocent this go-round."

A strand of her kinky hair was sticking out, making Rachel look like she'd just rolled out of bed. Laughing, Ian thumbed it away from her cheek, kissing her. In answer, she kissed him back with double the enthusiasm, then smiled to herself.

He wondered what kind of hidden thoughts that smile was entertaining, but even just guessing got him all stirred up again.

Yet before he went there, he needed to fire away with some questions. It was in his nature, having those niggling pokes of inquisitiveness erased.

"My assignment's almost finished," he said. "What do you think we should…?"

He couldn't continue. Good God, why not? He'd never been bashful about digging into anyone's business before.

She dropped her wooden spoon, and it clattered on the floor. With a nervous laugh, she picked it up, put it in the sink then got a new one. "What were you saying?"

All of a sudden, he was Mush Mouth, inarticulate.

While he dealt with this sudden impediment, she glanced curiously at him, transferred the vegetables to the plate and added more butter to the skillet, allowing it to melt. Then she held out her hands for Ian's egg bowl. As he gave it to her, their fingers met. The resulting charge that zigzagged into his hands reminded him of popcorn night, back when they'd first started getting to know each other.

Back when he'd been a confirmed bachelor and reporter.

She held the bowl, affected, too, her brows knitted. "I know what you're asking. 'Is it too soon to…'"

She widened her eyes and moved her head back and forth, substituting the confused gesture for words. Then she set down the bowl and removed the skillet from the burner, shutting the stove off.

"This is weird to talk about after one night, isn't it?" he asked, testing her.

She grinned, her gaze soft as she glanced at him. "I thought you were the straightforward one."

"Hey. I'm not a pro at this kind of thing."

"Right." She came over to rest her hands on his hips. "Usually you sprint out of bed before the crack of dawn, huh?"

Not quite, but it was close enough.

Running his hands up and down her arms, Ian imagined that this was their home, that they were going through the routine of waking up and starting their day, thinking of each other throughout the hours to sustain themselves until they returned to where they really wanted to be.

But that wasn't altogether right. He wanted to take her away, to make a new place for the both of them, someplace where they could start fresh with each other.

Rachel squeezed his waist, tickling him a little.

"I'm just going to come out with it," she said. "I wish you'd stay. I mean, there was a time I thought that men like you didn't come around but once in a blue moon, and I'm not too thrilled about letting you go."

He was surprised she'd put it out there, but impressed and relieved as well. "I don't want to go anywhere."

"Yeah?"

"Yeah."

Both of them laughed. *Thank God,* Ian thought. Maybe this love stuff was easier than they said.

Then it hit him.

Love.

Was that what had been screwing with his brain? The Holy Grail of emotion?

He hugged her to him, still hardly believing he'd stumbled upon it. Hadn't he?

And was he brave enough to claim it?

"Ian?" she asked.

He nuzzled the top of her head. "Mmm-hmm?"

"Where do you actually live? Albany?"

"I have an apartment there." Truthfully, he hadn't possessed a real home. Was Rachel wondering where they'd meet from now on? If he would actually quit his job and come here or if she would end up having to quit *her* job and leave her friends to be with him eventually?

So many ramifications.

I take it back, he thought. *This isn't easy after all.*

Just as they were getting to the crux of the situation, Ian's cell phone rang. He checked the number.

Nate Williams.

"How about this," he said before he answered. "We'll talk about the future after we clear all our work out of the way today. Okay?"

"Sounds like a plan."

And with a grin, she turned back around to the stove.

He took Nate's call, wondering how the hell a relationship infant like himself would survive all this plan-making with the woman he'd fallen for.

Chapter Eleven

Later that day, Gilbert was reeling.

As Jane walked him to the brown-brick Victorian campus house that he would be required to desert now that the university had fired him, he still couldn't believe what she had revealed while they were cleaning out his office.

"Are you all right?" she kept asking.

He merely kept nodding while they came closer and closer to his front porch.

But anyone could see that the sky was falling now that Gilbert was aware that his documents had been taken from his care.

All the same, he couldn't summon any genuine

anger about it. His ex-students had been doing what they thought was best for him by investigating. He could just imagine their own shock at having found what was in his safe.

No, it was too late to be angry. But it *was* clearly time to pay the piper for his sins.

As he and Jane paused by the stained-glass doorway, she said, "We don't have to do this interview, you know."

Interview. Gilbert laughed tightly. In the whirlpool of his grief, he had forgotten that Nate had arranged for Ian Beck to be here with the gang tonight, to celebrate Gilbert as the most unlikely hero in the history of time.

And…good Lord.

That meant Rachel would be here, as well.

The first bead of sweat popped onto his brow, and suddenly his collar and tie closed around his throat like a lynching mob's noose.

She has those adoption papers, he thought. *And she probably doesn't have any idea what to make of them, no idea why I, of all people, would have kept them in a safe.*

No wonder she had withdrawn from the gang around the time when, according to Jane, the documents had been taken.

Somehow, he had to find out what his favorite student was thinking, if she had the grace to forgive him. The mere hint that Rachel would hate him until the end of her days made Gilbert want to wither away and become nothing, just like one of the dying leaves that decorated his porch.

"Gilbert?" Jane asked. "I'll say it until I'm blue in the face. I'm sorry we had to—"

He shook his head, dismissing her apologies. She had been offering understandable explanations all afternoon, and he didn't deserve any of them.

"I suppose we shouldn't keep my guests any longer," he said, leading her into the foyer and avoiding the subject.

At least, for the time being.

Inside, the mumble of a small crowd greeted him. His living room was filled with the people he cared about the most: his ex-students. They mingled with one another while Ian Beck and his photographer prepared their equipment, including a video camera. Rachel lingered near the reporter, her hand on his waist as she smiled up at him.

She looked so joyful right now, and Gilbert's spirits sank as he realized that it certainly wasn't because of him.

When the gang saw their teacher, they greeted him with warmth and high cheer, trying to stabilize him after Jane's news, no doubt. But, finally, after everyone had said their piece, Rachel wandered over, looking as if she didn't know how to approach him.

Just who are you? she was probably thinking.

Sometimes, Gilbert didn't even know himself.

More sweat was causing his shirt to stick to his skin, and he loosened his collar, seeking relief.

"Hi," she said.

He couldn't stop obsessing about the documents.

She knew. Damn it all, she was waiting for an explanation that was years in the making.

And Gilbert wanted to tell all, even if he had shielded the truth merely to protect her from a confrontation such as this.

His stomach started to quake, tiny shivers of fear making him nauseous.

Before thinking, he opened his mouth to blurt out everything—to get it over and done with—but common sense throttled him. So did years of more justifications, reasons for keeping his secret from her.

"Listen," she said, searching his face, growing concerned at how he probably looked: pale, clammy and tortured. "If you want to talk privately after this interview, I'll be here." She took in a huge breath, and it trembled. "It's time I knew about a few things."

He could end the suspense now. Once again he started to speak, yet failed.

Dammit, Gilbert. Do it!

But he couldn't. Not now, maybe not ever. He couldn't even entertain the notion of being turned away by someone he wanted in his life so badly. Good Lord, it terrified him.

"All right, I guess it'll be later, then," she said, patently disappointed. She paused, seemingly to gather herself as she lifted her chin a notch. Even with the tough act, though, her gaze was infinitely gentle. "I only wish you would confide in me, Gilbert."

He managed a nod. A trickle of perspiration wiggled down his face, pooling on the top of his lip.

She was waiting for him to answer, but Gilbert's mouth was so dry he couldn't do it.

Say it, say it, say it...

She sighed. "I'm certainly open to whatever you have to tell me. *Finally* open." Here, her smile shined, as if she had made some sort of peace within herself. "It's just that...well, every time you helped me over the years, whether you were in benefactor mode or not, you never expected much back from me. I want you to know that I can do the same for you. Okay?"

"Rachel..." His voice was a croak.

Touching his arm in encouragement, she waited. But when the words didn't surface...*damn him*...she patted him instead.

"You don't look well. Do you need anything?"

By this time, Jane had rejoined him. "Gilbert?"

"No." He composed himself, adjusting his tie and collar. "I'm fine. Absolutely...fine."

"Then come along," Jane said, leading him away from Rachel and to his couch. "We're starting the interview. Is that okay with you?"

As Gilbert nodded, he saw a forlorn Rachel watching him leave, then making her way to her own seat, where she delicately crossed one leg over the other.

She seemed healthier somehow, more confident.

At some point, Ian Beck came over to thank Gilbert for this opportunity, but he barely registered it. Then the interview started, the video camera pointing at each of them in turn. Ian explained that the machine was there to help him keep track of everyone's answers since this was such a large crowd.

Everything twisted into a blur at that point for Gilbert. Sweat was smearing his eyesight, making Rachel's image bleed into a kaleidoscope of colors as he continually glanced at her. A low humming sound blocked his hearing as all the ex-students sang Gilbert's praises, telling Ian Beck what a heroic, and even flawed, figure their teacher was, defending him to the last.

His collar was choking the life out of him.

Say it, say it, say it...

In his bleary mind's eye, Rosemary, his sweet Rosemary, sat at her school secretarial desk on her very first day of work. She was wearing a tie-dyed shirt as she prepared for the fall semester. Her smooth, dark skin glimmered with perspiration because the air-conditioning was on the fritz. When Gilbert had introduced himself, she lit up the room with her smile.

He had lost his heart that day, lost his common sense and decency, as well, because loving Rosemary had turned his world upside down, had made him question everything.

Yet now, as Gilbert sat amid all the people he'd lied to, he took his punishment.

Smack. That was for cheating on his wife.

Smack, smack. That was for turning Rosemary aside when she needed him the most.

Smack, smack, smack. That was for hurting Rachel by hiding in plain sight from her when he knew that all she had ever wanted was to find her real family, even if she was afraid to do it.

A stilted laugh from the gang shook Gilbert into the moment, and he realized everyone in the room was staring at him, waiting for him to answer one of Ian Beck's questions. Rachel seemed as if she knew better though; she was halfway out of her chair, focusing on the sweat poring down his face.

And it didn't escape Gilbert's attention that, next to her, Cassidy and Ella were shooting him those knowing, pleading gazes.

Tell her. *Tell her!*

Ian Beck addressed Gilbert. "I'll repeat the question. Do you have any regrets about anything, Gilbert?"

Collar, choking. Sweat, drowning him.

"Yes." At the end of his rope, he pulled his tie all the way off. "I'm sorry I never spoke the truth."

"About being the benefactor," Beck clarified.

Even in his stupor, Gilbert could see that the reporter was watching Rachel, a protective set to his shoulders.

"I'm sorry about more than that," Gilbert said. "I'm also sorry that I never did right by Rachel's mother until now."

As the room went mortifyingly silent, Gilbert tried to stand up, but his legs gave out.

"Rachel," he barely managed to say as he fell back onto the couch.

She was by his side in a heartbeat. He tried to whisper to her, to absolve himself before he lost all control, to set himself free as Cassidy had urged him to do so many times.

To finally give Rosemary what she would have wanted for Rachel.

"I'm so very sorry," he said, his voice seeming to echo throughout the room. "I came close to telling you many times, but I thought I was sheltering the people I loved by staying quiet…."

"Shh, it's all right."

Rachel and Sandra eased him to his back. Everyone else gathered around him, calling Dr. Jacob Weber over to Gilbert's side.

All those horrified faces, staring down at him.

He was having trouble breathing now, so he spent his words carefully as he struggled to sit up.

"Those adoption papers. Rosemary…"

"She's my mom, I know. Please relax, Gilbert."

"No. I've got to tell you. She would have wanted me to…"

Rachel's face fell as she realized that Gilbert was telling her that Rosemary was dead.

He gasped for more oxygen. "Your father…there was an affair…."

Rachel's teary eyes went wide, filled with curious terror.

Gilbert steeled himself, then finally said it.

"It's me, Rachel. I'm your father."

Even though his heart was smashing against his ribs, he was already breathing easier. Lord help him, he had relieved his soul.

Hope creeping into his heart, Gilbert risked a smile, his mouth quivering at the corners as he wished she would burst into a smile, too.

But as her eyes went blank and still, all Gilbert's best scenarios crisped to ash.

Was his greatest fear coming true, right before his eyes?

Was Rachel the daughter who didn't want him?

In that moment, the earth stopped spinning for Rachel.

How weird, she thought, sitting in her bubble of timeless silence, still absorbing his words. She hadn't known how the revelation would make her feel, but it wasn't like this. Numb, removed, emotionless.

Her real mom was dead. Rachel would never know her or hear her side of this…this…

Affair, he'd said. Was he validating that, not only was she unwanted, but she was illegitimate, a source of shame?

Suddenly, a series of camera flashes burst her protective bubble, and she closed her stinging eyes, lifting up her arm to block her face.

And, just as if someone had pressed the play button,

life went into motion again, furious sounds flooding her ears as Ian jerked his cameraman away from the group. He started to yell at Joe, but all Rachel heard was white noise.

Even the moving mouths of the friends who were hugging her weren't producing anything that made sense.

Gilbert was staring at her, his face mirroring her own shock. He wasn't having a heart attack or stroke as she had feared. In fact, he'd stopped sweating altogether.

And she had started.

Pinpricks of panicked heat.

Feeling ill, she lurched to her feet, ignoring everybody as she rushed to the door and outside, not knowing where she was going, where she was running off to.

All she knew was that she had to withdraw before it got worse. Because it would. It always did.

As she ran and ran, her space bubble, her tried-and-true method of survival, formed around her again, just as it had when she was a girl. No one could get to Rachel inside the bubble—not her adoptive parents knocking on her bedroom door to punish her. Not the kids at school who made fun of her "cave-girl" hair. Not Gilbert, who had listened to her go on and on about her natural parents and how she was scared spitless to look for them.

There'd been so many times that she'd wished for a father like Gilbert—heck, that she'd wished Gilbert *was* her dad. And when she'd seen the adoption papers, she'd even fantasized for a fleeting moment that he was the man who belonged in the mysterious space that read Father: Unknown. But then she'd stopped thinking that way, because the big question proved too agonizing.

If he were her dad, why hadn't he told her?

The answer was simple. It would've meant that he didn't want her at all.

So she'd shoved the suspicion out of her mind, never acknowledging it again, telling herself it was silly and impossible.

Exhausted now, she stopped running, coming to a lone oak tree at the edge of campus and sinking against the trunk. She realized that tears were bathing her face, that her chest was heaving with sobs.

Part of her wanted to go back to the house and hear Gilbert out. But the other part of her argued that he'd had a lot of chances to explain already and there was a reason he'd kept his silence.

A reason she couldn't bear to hear.

He'd said that he wanted to shelter the people he loved, and that was bull. Complete and utter bull. No excuse could be good enough for keeping the truth away from her, lying to her by omission all these years and setting her up for such a crash.

As Rachel drew into herself, she realized that there was one truth in life: no matter what you did, everyone abandoned you. Natural parents, husbands, people who made excuses for never claiming you as their own.

But, she thought, drying her tears, she knew the trick to surviving. She'd learned it very, very well.

You had to abandon people first, before they destroyed you altogether.

That was the one fact she could depend on.

When Rachel had escaped, Ian had been too busy busting Joe's balls to keep tabs. Consequently, when he finally sprinted out the door after her, she'd already disappeared.

When he returned soon afterward, he found that some of the other members of the gang were looking for her, too, while the other half stayed with Gilbert.

David Westport had ushered Ian back inside the house. "We'll be here for her when she's ready."

But that wasn't good enough for Ian. And he realized that he had another problem on his hands, too.

Joe, who had been taking pictures of Rachel just after Gilbert's confession. As a reporter, Ian knew the photos were priceless: they'd shown the naked vulnerability on her face, the profound loneliness of a woman who was surrounded by friends yet had no one to turn to.

The story had exploded into a disaster, and all that was left to do was clean up the remains.

Dr. Jacob Weber was checking over a mournful Gilbert. The rest of the gang was attempting to get their teacher to explain himself, even though Gilbert felt he owed his reasoning to Rachel first and foremost.

Ian did his own part, cornering Joe outside. His next task would be to take off after Rachel again. He was too worried about her to sit here and do nothing.

"Give me the camera," Ian said.

The photographer laughed, obviously thinking that Ian was kidding around. But his abrupt halt of gaiety signaled a realization that Ian was dead serious.

"Don't be ridiculous," Joe said. "This story just gets better and better. Edgar the Evil Editor is going to give us both raises because of this, you lunkhead."

Maybe Ian was too protective of Rachel now, but it felt right being that way. "Remember what we talked about? Bringing out the positive side of Gilbert's struggles?"

"Aw, God, I saw it happening but it's done gone and become a fact." Joe cradled his camera. "She's messed with your head, partner, and you'd better fix it quick, because you're not acting like a professional anymore."

As Joe yammered on, Ian took a step back. Is this how he'd acted, too? Had he been so distanced from his stories that they'd meant nothing to him? Had he seen so much anguish that the tragedy had become just another part of his day?

"Hey," Joe said. "Don't look at me like that. You might want to piss off the editor by pushing his buttons with your sudden taste for 'heroes' and 'peace' and 'love,' but I took this assignment only because it was a slice of pie, Ian. You did, too, at first. Come next week, we'll be on another story, and Saunders University and your affair will be left in the dust."

Dust. Yeah, Ian did feel dirtied. Compromised.

But it didn't have to be that way.

Not anymore.

He thought of what was in that camera: reflections of Rachel's worst nightmares. The world had no business being a part of that.

It was up to him to preserve her dignity.

"I'm going to ask you one last time," Ian said. "Nicely."

Joe's eyes darted here and there—anywhere but on Ian.

"Give. Me. The. Camera."

Body tensing, the photographer vehemently shook his head. Then his gaze finally narrowed on his co-worker. "Once, you were the best. But you've lost it. What a waste."

Ian smiled and *not* nicely. "And thank God for that."

A tense second was the only buffer between them. But after it passed, Ian made a successful grab for the camera.

Joe sprinted away, hell for leather, and within seconds Ian found out why.

The cameraman had already secured the film.

And when Ian checked the video equipment, he found that those contents were absent, too.

Ian cursed, then went back outside and tossed the machinery into the bushes, caring less about the cost.

But, hell. He knew what to do. He'd give Copley Willens, the owner of the *National Sun,* a call to see if he could block Joe's pictures. If not, then Ian would put in his resignation.

Or...

He smiled to himself.

Actually, he was going to put in his damned walking papers, anyway.

Ian turned back around to get his jacket. But that's when something caught his eye.

Rachel, wandering down the opposite street from where Joe had gone, her arms closed over her chest as if warding off the world.

Without hesitation, he went to her, leaving the pursuit of Joe and the pictures alone, deserting his story.

Certain that his real job was to take care of the woman he loved.

The truth sang in him, giving him confidence and optimism. He walked at a faster clip, gaining momentum with every step.

If working for the *National Sun* included hurting her, he wanted no part of it. Reporting wasn't what powered him now.

Rachel was.

He caught up to her, blocking her progress, holding her arms and bending down to catch her eye.

"Gilbert's house is that way," he said gently.

She stopped walking. When she glanced at him, her eyes were tear-filled, her cheeks streaked with red. Ian wanted to hold her to him and say everything would be okay, because it would be. He'd make sure of it.

"How is he?" she asked.

"Shaken."

She huffed out a breath. Still, her slumped shoulders were bearing more weight than she should be handling alone.

"Ready to come with me?" he asked.

"I'm not going back."

He hesitated. "All right. Maybe not today. Everyone will understand. You were dealt a heavy blow."

At the reminder, she flinched, then moved away from him.

Hands empty, Ian didn't know what to do. He was talking to a stranger, not the woman he'd made love with last night. Not the Rachel who'd laughed with him while making omelets in her kitchen. Not the one whom he suspected might feel the same love that he did.

"Rachel?" he asked.

"You should go back to the house, Ian. You have to wind up the interview."

"I'm not publishing it. But I have a bad feeling that the pictures might make it, and Joe can write an eyewitness account of Gilbert's confession himself."

Rachel's heart sank. Hopelessness surrounded her, caving her in. She could see the headlines now: *Naughty Professor Tells All About Abandoned Bastard Child.*

"You're not writing an article?" she managed to ask.

"No."

He was watching her with such affection that it was serrating her, reducing her to bits and pieces that couldn't ever be fit back together again.

See? Pain. Love was just a noble word to describe why it hurt so much when people disappointed you.

She couldn't look at him, because all she wanted to do was fall against him, to depend on him way too much. And if she did that now, it would just be worse when he *did* end up leaving her.

Because he would. In spite of the talk they'd had this morning, the sunny peek into a brighter future, he would find some excuse to pack his bags and reject her.

They all did.

Abandon him before he abandons you said a voice in the back of her mind.

And, from what little Rachel now knew, the voice belonged to Rosemary, who'd also been set aside by a man. A woman who was—now more than ever—very much alive in Rachel's mind, even if she was long gone.

"I've been thinking." She swallowed heavily, bit her lip then forced herself to recover. "We really jumped into things, Ian. I think we should be clear about what last night really was."

His expression fell. "And what was that?"

Her throat burned. She couldn't do this.

But she had to. Survival demanded it.

"Fun. Games." Fortifying herself, Rachel shrugged,

pretending this wasn't bringing her to her emotional knees. "You don't have to be nice about it, Ian. I know you've got a girl in every port."

"Not this time." He came over, took her by the arms as if to keep her from fleeing. "Rachel, I…"

She held her breath. If he said it, she was going to disintegrate, lose all the memories that were guiding her and holding her solid. But she could see that she'd already planted some doubt in his mind, that he was wondering if he'd jumped to conclusions during their speedy relationship.

Hurry, Rosemary, the invisible conscience, said, *before he realizes he's wrong and sucks you into something that'll become even worse than it is now.*

"Truthfully," she said, fighting the ache that was stinging her chest, her throat, her jaw, "you've made my life a media circus. You had a heavy hand in putting my private pain on display, Ian. That's hard to accept."

Lie. Liar, liar, liar.

His grip tightened on her arms. "I'm not after a story now. I haven't been for a while."

With the last of her strength, she stared into his eyes, contradicting him, playing on what had to be his worst fears, too.

Damn her. Damn all of this. She knew her excuses were chipping away at him.

Rescuing her.

As a final push, she summoned her swan song. Her

acting talents. President of the Drama Club. Star of the school play.

Until she quit halfway through, of course.

"We had a good time together, didn't we?" she asked. "So let's leave it at that. You go on with your life and I'll go on with mine."

As she spoke, he started to shake his head, denying it. "Don't talk like this, Rachel. Don't…"

"Best of luck, okay?" Her voice cracked, just like the earth opening up to swallow her whole. "I had a lot of fun."

Then she started walking away before she lost her guts, before she gave in and caused even deeper grief for herself.

Ian's voice rang over the cold air. "You can't withdraw this time, Rachel."

She whipped around. He was raising up his palms, as if pleading with her. She tried to shut him out of her heart—the man who'd charmed her with his blue eyes, winning smile and tender caresses.

"This is more than withdrawal," she said, performing her encore. "So don't call…." Tears gushed in her eyes. "Don't e-mail…." Then rolled down her face. *"Don't bother."*

When his hands lowered in defeat, his face a mask of heartbreak, Rachel turned around and ran.

Faster. Faster.

Escaping.

Heading back to all the demons who'd kept her safe—until this point.

Chapter Twelve

Early December snow drifted outside the window of Ian's New York apartment, a place he'd moved in to just days before. In front of him, a laptop's screen blinked as if it were a child, ready to be fed with thoughts and stories.

And he'd written a few of them since leaving Boston a couple of weeks ago.

For about the zillionth time, he glanced at the cell phone on his desk. Rachel was a call away, but whenever he remembered this, his heart seemed to disappear that much more.

Their last meeting replayed in his head, haunting him, because every doubt he'd possessed about his inability to commit had come to a head. He'd questioned the reality of his emotions for Rachel after she'd pushed him away. He'd wondered if he was capable of more than one-night flings.

Over and over he told himself that he shouldn't have listened to her, that he should've run after her when she'd abandoned him. After all, her rejection of Ian had come from Gilbert's own treatment of *her.*

And that's what got to Ian the most—because if he had really loved Rachel, he could've overcome her knee-jerk reaction. He could've risen above it and had the fortitude to stay the course in his emotions.

Yet, being the ultimate bachelor, he hadn't had any practice in saving relationships. And after Joe's pictures and article had been published in the *National Sun*… Hell, the "media circus" Rachel had accused him of creating became all too real.

She'd been right, Ian thought. He'd only brought more trouble into her existence, and leaving her in the comfort of her friends' circle had been the best choice, after all.

Bottom line? He was respecting her wishes to be left alone, he thought, coming back to the least-painful excuse.

Or was that just his guilt talking? Had he made her life better or *worse* by leaving?

Dammit, if only he could have a second chance, he'd…

What? Try again? Stick by her side and see her through the worst of times?

Hell, yeah, he would.

His chest ached, but not because of any physical reason. It was because he was helpless under a love that had only grown with distance and what-ifs.

His computer winked at him again.

Work, he thought. *Get back to it. It might make you feel better.*

So he did, pounding out a draft for his new assignment, even though labor never *did* fully erase the regrets. Since quitting the paper, Ian had been freelancing, scouring the country and seeking out heroes to write about. It had kept him busy.

And it had brought him attention.

Copley Willens, the owner of the *National Sun,* had persuaded Ian to work for him in another capacity. He'd said Ian had too much talent to waste and had lured him with the opportunity to create the sort of stories he wanted.

It should've made Ian feel better. And it did.

As much as it could, anyway.

Now he was the newest "color reporter" on the staff of *Up and About,* the U.S.'s number-one-rated TV morning show. Besides continuing his freelance work, Ian was contracted to present a weekly portrait of American spirit, the best of what the country had to offer.

He was proficient at it, too, finding everyday miracles in places like a country diner where the so-called town drunk had performed CPR on the police chief who had persecuted him for a decade. Or on the side of a road where a wheelchair-bound boy had ventured out of his house to save the life of an old man who'd crashed his car into a ditch.

Reporting about the cream of humanity was rescuing Ian from self-destruction, even though he was missing one important piece of himself.

Rachel.

Shoving away from his desk, Ian gave up, standing from his chair, denying his work. He had to get back to her. He had to tell Rachel that he loved her and wanted to be with her for the rest of his life.

But how? How could he prove that nothing else mattered but the way they felt about each other?

As Ian paced the room, ignoring his deadline, he realized that the most heroic thing *he* could ever do would be to throw caution to the wind.

But how could he do that without being sensitive to what she'd asked of him?

Beaten for the moment, Ian sat back down, preparing himself for a long night of plotting and planning.

A long night of asking himself if Rachel would ever open her heart to him again.

The next morning, Boston fell under the same gentle storm, snow lightly frosting the sidewalk in front of Rachel's house as she waited for the guest she'd finally invited over.

Inside, she had a fire going. Near it stood a small

plastic Christmas tree, reminding her that it was "that time of year"—a season in which families came together. And this Christmas, more than others, she was keenly reminded that she didn't have anyone to celebrate with.

She was estranged from her adoptive family. She hadn't seen Gilbert since the blowout. She was too buried under her new full-time status at the firm to visit much with the gang. And Ian...

Rachel placed a hand over her chest, soothing the terrible anguish. It didn't do any good to revisit her regrets. He'd moved on with a new job and had probably gotten over her already.

The part about the job she knew for certain. She'd watched his premiere on *Up and About,* read every article that he'd published from the road.

But had he found another woman?

The suggestion crushed her. She was a masochist for dwelling on it.

An expected knock on her door brought Rachel to her feet. When she peered out the window to verify who it was, her nerves came to attention.

She opened the door for Gilbert, his dark overcoat iced with bits of snow.

"Hi," she said, ushering him inside. "I'm glad you came."

"Hello, Rachel."

He took off his black fedora and held it in his hands as she shut the door. God, he was so pale, a ghost of what he used to be. Bags weighed under his eyes, which were bleary and hopeless.

Rachel knew she looked the same way, too, except she, at least, had a job to help her hide, to deal with all the mistakes she'd made.

Yup, she thought. *My own sedative of choice comes in the package of legal briefs and research. Nice.*

Gilbert couldn't stop staring at her, and Rachel fidgeted under the apologetic scrutiny.

"Can I take your hat and coat?" she asked, not knowing what else to say, even though she'd been rehearsing and dreading this day for a couple of weeks.

But the events of these last few months had taught her that she would have to face her problems. That meant she needed to actually call Gilbert and invite him over to talk. The approach of Christmas had only intensified the yearning to finally make amends with the man who'd lied to her, to eventually contact her adoptive parents and talk things out with them, too.

It took a few more worldless minutes to get Gilbert settled. He refused coffee or tea, instead choosing to take a seat on the couch by the fire.

Finally, he spoke. "I waited to contact you out of respect. The gang told me you weren't willing to see me, so I was hoping you would make the first gesture."

She sat on a chair opposite him. "I was afraid that if I talked to you any sooner than this, it would've gotten ugly. I wasn't ready. But then Christmas started rolling around…."

Shrugging, she didn't bother to explain when they both knew what she was talking about. Nobody wanted to spend the holiday alone, especially when you needed to make up with someone out there who said they cared about you.

The image of an arrogant grin and piercing blue eyes flashed before her.

Pain gripped Rachel's heart, her stomach. Ian. She'd tried so hard to put him out of her head, her very soul, because she still believed it was the best option in the long run. Wasn't it?

So why was she reaching out to Gilbert, who had already betrayed her, and not to Ian, who only had the potential to wound her?

Reluctantly, she put him out of her mind, but he lingered there, anyway, suffusing her entire body with a bone-deep longing for him.

Gilbert was gauging her, and she glanced toward the fire.

He laughed bitterly, as if acknowledging that he was being punished. "What can I do to make it up to you? How can I make you realize how sincere I am about regretting what I did?"

"I don't have the energy to punish you."

"I understand." His voice was shaking.

When she found enough courage to glance at him, she saw that a tear was running down his face. Guilt flooded her, because she didn't want it to be this way.

"Will you explain everything?" she asked, fighting

the urge to sit next to him, to hug him or comfort him like she used to. "I'd really like to hear your reasons now."

He reached up to wipe away the tear, nodding. "I've gone over this in my head so many times, but none of it sounds good enough."

"Please?" she asked. "Try?"

"Yes. I'll do more than try." Now it was his turn to focus on the fire. The tears glimmered on his face. "You know her name. Rosemary Johnson. She was a secretary at Saunders, a beautiful woman who turned all the heads in our department."

He reached into his wallet and brought out a picture. It showed a gorgeous woman, her skin a smooth cocoa, her smile wide and trusting. She was sitting at a desk and posing for the camera, but Rachel realized that there was something about her brown-tinted gaze… As if Gilbert had taken the picture and she was sending him a hundred messages of quiet love with her eyes.

Rachel couldn't look away, because she also felt that Rosemary was communicating with her, too, connecting with her from heaven. "What was she like?"

"Gentle-natured, funny. She had a contagious laugh you could hear all the way down the hall, where I would listen and smile. She was always having a good time, even when everyone else was in a bad mood. She had what George Bernard Shaw called a 'life force,' a quality that holds a person in thrall. She would have been a wonderful mother."

So Rosemary laughed a lot, just like Isaac. Like Ian, too. Strange, how both Rachel and Gilbert were drawn to happiness. Like father, like… Rachel shoved the thought to the back of her mind.

"And your wife?" A thread of anger crept into Rachel's voice as she thought about the woman who had kept Gilbert's home for so many years. The woman who had died with her husband's name on her lips. "What about Mary?"

"I loved her, too, Rachel, but not in the same way. Mary was comfortable, like a favorite sweater that warms you up. Rosemary…"

His voice trailed off, but he didn't have to go on. Rachel felt the same way about Ian.

"She was your everything," Rachel said.

And you couldn't get enough of her, she added silently. Without her, everything lost its color, like red fading to a washed-out pink.

"At first," Gilbert said, "I didn't act on my feelings, but I could tell Rosemary was much too aware of me, as well. Then, one night at a staff gathering, we found ourselves alone, talking. We had so much in common, but she broadened my world with her perspective, too. She had grown up in the South, and she had such stories about her family, her way of life down there. She was a fighter, a free spirit."

Without even meeting her, Rachel knew that she would've idolized her mother. She would've wanted to be just like her.

"After that," Gilbert added, "we started to meet for lunch. Then dinner. Then…it happened, and neither of us could stop ourselves."

"Did Mary ever know?"

Gilbert seemed horrified. "No. Never. The last thing I wanted to do was hurt her. I believed, or I *justified,* that divorce would humiliate my wife. I thought she would suffer much more if she knew about Rosemary than if she remained blissfully unaware. Of course, I worried about losing my job as well…"

Here, Rachel got a hint of Gilbert's system of reasoning, because she had no doubt that he'd applied the same line of thought to her situation, too. She could try to understand it, but that didn't make it right. Not by a long shot.

He seemed to guess what was going through Rachel's head. "I know I was wrong. But we all tell ourselves little lies, Rachel, and that's how we survive."

Her belly constricted, and she tried not to think of Ian. But she did. He wasn't ever far from her.

So how could she fault Gilbert when she was telling herself lies, too?

"I felt as if I couldn't leave my wife for Rosemary," Gilbert continued as he sank back into the couch, seemingly exhausted, "even if that's all I wanted to do. And it wasn't only because of my warped protection of Mary's feelings. Times were different back then, even around this area. Society wasn't as tolerant of a white man loving a black woman. Both Rosemary and I were concerned about being targeted. And when she got pregnant with you, we were saddened by the reality of how a mixed-heritage baby would be treated, as well."

"Was it any worse than what I did end up enduring?" she asked.

"I didn't plan for you to end up in a tense family situation." Gilbert rested his forehead in his hands, probably because he was unable to meet her searching gaze. "If I would have known…"

He seemed so genuine that she actually believed he would change things if he could. Why? Heaven help her, she was ten kinds of fool.

"I'm not proud of myself," Gilbert said. "In fact, I've tried to make up for what I've done."

Then it hit her. "The benefactor? You thought mentoring kids and giving money away to others in need would wash away what you did with Rosemary?"

"Yes, my gifts were a payment of my debt. I wanted to improve the lives of people who were faced with adversity or unfair choices. I'd hoped to redeem myself—not end my career." He shook his head. "But the remorse never left. What happened after Rosemary got pregnant barred me from any redemption."

He fisted a handful of his hair and, automatically, Rachel got up to comfort him. It was beyond her to watch this frail man undergo such inner torture, no matter how much he deserved it. But hadn't he tried to make up for what he'd done? Didn't that count for something?

She sat next to him, removing his hand from his hair, but she didn't keep a hold of him. Rachel was too caught between disgust and pity to even know how to react.

"Please tell me the rest," she whispered, almost afraid to hear.

A tiny sob wrenched out of him and she gave in, resting her hand on his back. Her touch seemed to calm him, to bring him back from a personal hell.

"When we learned Rosemary was pregnant, it jolted me. I ended the relationship and gave her money to set up life in a new city, a place where she could get a fresh start. I told myself you both would never lack for anything, that I would always support you."

"You treated her like a kept woman. And you treated me—"

Although she couldn't say it, the words rang loud and clear throughout her conscience: *You treated me like I wasn't good enough.*

Gilbert sat up. "I thought it was for the best, Rachel. I intended to keep in touch with you both, and I desperately tried, but Rosemary cut off all contact."

It was on the tip of her tongue to say that she didn't blame Rosemary, but Rachel couldn't do it. Not when Gilbert was so racked with grief. She wasn't cruel enough to plunge him deeper into depression, even though a part of her wanted to strike out and wound him as thoroughly as he'd done to her and her mother.

"So you never heard from her again?" she asked.

"Just once. She sent me an anonymous note written on plain paper when you were born. At that point, everything became clear to me. I wanted my child, so I set out to find you."

"You did?" Rachel asked, starting to cry.

He'd wanted her. *Someone* had needed her.

"Yes." Tentatively, Gilbert smiled. "I hired a P.I. to find you and Rosemary, but by then it was too late. You'd been adopted and couldn't be traced. Rosemary had passed away due to pneumonia. Still, I tried to keep track of your whereabouts. And the investigator had secured a copy of your adoption papers and I kept them, just as a reminder of what I'd done wrong, what I needed to correct if I ever had the chance. I had to hide them in my office safe because I didn't want Mary to discover them."

Her chest felt heavy, as if her heart were full of tears that needed to be shed. "And Mary never did find out?"

"Never. From that day on, I devoted myself to her and she never suspected a thing."

"Oh, poor Mary." And Rosemary.

"One day," he said, wiping at his eyes, "by chance, I came upon a college application from 'Rachel James' while I was working on the admissions committee. Some of the information matched what the P.I. had uncovered about you and, with a little more work and a few greased palms, he confirmed that you were my daughter. That's how you received the financial package, Rachel. And when you finally accepted the offer

I'd put together from Saunders, I couldn't believe it. Then I became your guidance counselor and what I thought of as your surrogate parent. My happiness knew no bounds. The only dark spot was that you didn't know I was your father—and I had the power to wash away all your sadness with that one confession."

"Why didn't you tell me then?"

He hesitated, giving her ample time to rethink everything that had happened between them: how he'd reacted when her marriage had taken her away from school and *him*. How he'd tried in vain to get her back to Saunders.

He'd wanted any excuse to have a relationship with her. There was no doubting that.

"I have a lot of reasons for my silence," he finally said. "On the surface, I believed the news about Rosemary would put my career in jeopardy, which was all I felt that I had left, on most days. But maybe I was really keeping the truth from you out of pure shame. I knew you would despise me for my choices, and the thought of that killed me, Rachel. I couldn't give you one more reason to withdraw from life, even if it pulled me apart to watch you battling through each week."

She found herself nodding, even though it would take time to fully comprehend his reasons. But the thing was, she was willing to do that now.

It was simpler than she'd expected.

And much more complicated.

"There're no clear-cut answers for what you did,

Gilbert." Hesitantly, she took his hands in hers, the Christmas tree hovering in back of him. It was a sign of grace and forgiveness. "But I think it might be time to sort through what's happened."

"Or start over, using all the mistakes as a lesson."

This time, she started *really* crying, heaving gulps of relief and hope. Gilbert hugged her, soothing her as a true father would.

What he did, she thought, he did for everyone around him. He sincerely cares about all of us...cares about me. Sure, he was playing God, but he was thinking of his loved ones while doing it.

In the end, losing Gilbert because she couldn't give him another chance just seemed so petty.

Rachel stopped crying and suddenly sat up. Losing *anyone* for that reason was wrong.

She had to get Ian back, too, no matter the cost.

"I've made a lot of mistakes myself," she said, easing back into the groove of mentor-student. Except, in time, maybe theirs could be a different—and similar—relationship.

Father and daughter.

"Why, what have you done?" He sounded so grateful now, so overjoyed at the possibility of having his daughter accept him.

She laughed, realizing that she was allowed to be happy, realizing that she *could* right the other wrongs as well.

Then she thought of Ian. "I chased someone away.

Someone I love. And it was because of fear. But I don't know if I'll ever be able to make it up to him."

"Ian Beck." Gilbert laughed at Rachel's surprise. "You couldn't hide *that*."

Since the wheels of her mind had been spinning for so long, working up scenarios in which she showed Ian just how sorry she was, the process of getting them running again wasn't an effort. She had no clue if he would ever forgive her for driving him away, but she wanted to try. Needed to try with every cell of her being.

"We have to get both of our lives back on track," she said. "Could we talk about what we're going to do now? Could we look ahead instead of backward for the time being?"

Even though she knew they'd never forget the past, she wanted to barge forward, to start a new day. It was Christmas, after all. A new beginning.

"You want to help me?" he asked, obviously touched.

Rachel smiled. "Despite everything, you've helped *me* a lot over the years, and I want to return the favor. You're too valuable to have no purpose."

A spark of the old Gilbert—the enthusiastic professor they all loved—flared in his brown eyes.

Santa lives, she thought, rejoicing.

"Count me in on the brainstorming," he said.

"Then let me put on some coffee and music." Carols, sweet tunes, uplifting melodies.

She also intended to call the gang to see what they

could come up with for the future. They would want to be a part of getting Gilbert back on track, too.

"But first…" Rachel said.

She stuck out her hand. "We need to try a new start, to see if things can work. Hi. I'm Rachel."

For a second, he looked at her outstretched palm. Then, with all the warmth of the love she'd missed while growing up, he clasped his hand in hers, treasuring it with a light squeeze.

"Glad to meet you," he said, a tear in his eye. "I'm your father."

The next night, Ian got a call from the assistant he'd worked with at the *National Sun*. She'd told him some very interesting news: the ghost of Christmas past was getting some sweet retribution.

After students and teachers had protested the treatment of Professor Harrison, Alex Broadstreet had come under review for how he'd handled the hearings.

Hah! Ian thought. *Would I ever like to be back in Boston for this.*

But as soon as he remembered the city, the Old State House, the little bookstore where he and Rachel had gotten to know each other…well, he lost heart.

Dammit, where had all his guts gone? Why couldn't he put any of his grand plans to sweep Rachel off her feet into motion?

His cell phone rang, and without even consulting the calling screen, he answered it.

"Beck."

There was silence, then a voice. "Ian?"

The room seemed to tilt, as if Ian's vision had gone wacko. His body felt the same way. "Rachel."

"It's me, all right." She laughed. "If you want to hang up now, you can."

Was she kidding? He'd been thinking of so many excuses to call her that he could've wallpapered this building with a list of them.

Still, he tried to play it cool. His heart couldn't take another beating like the one she'd already administered. "How have you been?"

"Better. Much, much better, but…"

He was holding his breath.

"I really miss you," she said.

Ian almost fell out of his chair as she continued.

"But I want to apologize to you in person, Ian. I can't do it over the phone. Not if I have any integrity at all."

Was she inviting him back there? The crazy-in-love half of him was ready to pack his bags. But the smart, heartbroken half held him back.

"Ian?"

He cleared his throat. "Yeah?"

"I've also got an offer for you."

Okay. Maybe he'd been wise to be a little wary. "An offer."

"Right. I've been talking to the gang again, and we've been watching your hero pieces on *Up and About*. We'd like you to consider coming over here for an interview with Gilbert—an exclusive. He's decided to help the Westports run their children's sports camp, and we think he'd make a perfect story for you."

Ian's hopes folded up. So this *was* just business?

He sat down again. "I don't know, Rachel. I was thinking of coming to Boston to freelance Alex Broadstreet's story, but—"

"I've got to see you again." She'd blurted it out. "Please? I'm sorry for everything. I just want the chance to talk, okay?"

Not only was Ian intrigued, he was so damned smitten that wild horses wouldn't be able to keep him from going to Boston now.

Did he have no pride?

Nope. "I'll arrange a flight. But, Rachel?"

"Yes?" It sounded as if she was dancing around the room or something.

He grew serious. "Don't stage a repeat of last time, because I can't take it."

The line went quiet for the slightest moment before she came back on.

"I'm going to make it up to you," she said. "I promise."

When they hung up, Ian realized something scary.

He'd just positioned himself as a big red target for love to whup his ass yet again.

But…what the hell. He was going to go for it, rejection or not.

She was worth every growing pain.

Chapter Thirteen

When Ian's flight landed, he expected to travel directly to his hotel, meet his camera crew in the morning and then see Rachel before he returned to Saunders to cover the Alex Broadstreet story. He would be conducting Gilbert's interview the day after.

But that's not quite how it turned out.

As he headed with his carry-on bag toward the terminal exit, he saw a familiar face holding a sign with his name on it.

David Westport, one of the gang.

Weird, Ian thought, going over to the ex-athlete. Why was David acting like a chauffeur?

The other man greeted Ian with an embarrassed grin, his skin ruddy as they shook hands. "Welcome back."

"Thanks." Ian tried not to seem too miffed about Rachel sending a friend instead of showing up here herself. Maybe this *had* been all about the interview the gang had set up for Gilbert later tomorrow.

Maybe Rachel hadn't meant anything personal by that phone call….

Dammit. Ian tried to hold it together, to pretend that his last wish for reconciliation hadn't just fizzled.

"Now, man to man," David said, "I'm going to warn you about what's coming up, all right?"

Here it is, Ian thought. *The part where Rachel officially slices me in half again, except this time by proxy.*

"Spit it out," he said, his hand fisting around the strap of his travel bag.

Much to Ian's bafflement, a sheepish David brought out a gift from behind his sign.

A mini bunny in a Red Sox uniform, just like the one he'd bought for his nieces and nephews.

Perplexed, Ian accepted the stuffed animal from David, realizing that there was a tiny note hanging from a string around the bunny's waist.

"This is what I'm supposed to say." David rolled his eyes, but he was still smiling. "'Read the signs and follow your heart.' Jeez, I can't believe that just came out of my mouth."

Even though David was being difficult, Ian could tell that he was enjoying this. For his own part, however, Ian didn't know exactly how to feel.

He was too cautious. Too confused about Rachel's intentions.

David pointed to the bunny's note. "You have to look at it in order to get anywhere. And...listen. If you're worried, don't be. I'm not supposed to give anything away except that Rachel wants to prove something to you, got it?"

Sure, Ian wanted to have faith in that. So did his heart, which was pitter-pattering, going from a wary tiptoe to a tentative lope through his chest.

Resting his hand on his bag, Ian thought about what was inside—something shiny and beautiful captured in a square velvet box.

Because his own dreams had never died.

As David looked on, Ian read the note, which was written in neat, tiny letters: *I used to carry a lot of baggage, Ian, but I've let it go. It's time I held on to something more worthwhile.*

That's when his pulse began to jog.

"Baggage claim?" Ian asked, revving up to take off.

David nodded, his smile widening. "Go get her."

Ian didn't have to be told twice. As his heart went from that jog to a full-out run, he sprinted toward his next destination.

In the background, he heard David yell, "And thanks again for the interview!"

Already out of breath, Ian waved and took a corner at about one hundred miles per hour.

Dodging, running, leaping over a suitcase someone

had rested on the floor, he made Baggage Claim in record time.

But when he got there, he only saw strangers waiting for their luggage. No Rachel.

What…?

Someone tapped his shoulder from behind.

Bursting into a huge grin, Ian turned around, ready to greet the woman he loved.

But it was David's wife, Sandra Westport.

"Sorry to disappoint," she said, a glimmer of mischief in her gaze.

"I'm not…" Sigh.

Okay. He couldn't deny it. His stomach had sunk to the floor.

She gave him another bunny, and he knew just what to do.

I know I drove you crazy, read the note, *but when I told you that we didn't have anything special, I was lying, especially to myself. I'm so sorry, Ian.*

Rachel hadn't meant a word of what she'd said when she'd turned him away? Had their time together marked her for life as it had him?

Ian laughed, joy pumping through him.

Sandra mock-whispered to him. "See the clue? '*Drove* you crazy'?"

"Transportation counter." Ian didn't waste another second. And when he arrived there, he found Jane Jackson.

"Don't tell me I'll have to wade through all of you,"

he said, his desire to see Rachel again reaching critical
mass. "Not that I'm unhappy to see you, but—"

She gave him his bunny. "You're almost there."

Tearing into this note, he read it with superhuman
speed.

*I want you back more than anything on this earth,
and I hope you'll forgive me. When I'm with you, I
know I can forget my past, because thoughts of the future are so bright.*

He stood there for a moment, his throat working as
he fought emotion. To buy time, he unzipped his bag
and put the bunnies inside. They nestled next to the velvet box he was carrying.

A box that held their shining future.

Finally, he got a hold of himself, the need to see
Rachel again raging, churning, blasting inside of him.

Jane had tears in her eyes. "She couldn't figure out
how to put another clue in that note, so…" She pointed
over Ian's shoulder. "Go to a bar called Tina and Ikey's.
You'll find the next step there…if you want to take it."

By now, Ian could barely see or listen, because his
heartbeat was owning him, muddling his sight and his
hearing. But he managed to make it to the bar, anyway.

There, what he found made him stop in the entrance,
overwhelmed with a feeling so mysteriously awesome
that it defied his experience.

Rachel was sitting at a table, anxiety written all over
her face as she waited for him. She was wearing a Red
Sox cap, just like the bunnies, and holding her own note.

When she saw him, her lips parted and her gaze softened. She stood, holding up her sign.

I never stopped loving you, Ian Beck.

Without a thought to propriety, he dashed over to her, sweeping her into his arms and embracing her, kissing her until they both almost stumbled to the ground.

God, her perfume. The familiarity of her hair against his cheek, the slope of her body pressed against his, the warmth of her skin.

"I love you, too," he said, never wanting to let her go. "I never stopped. If you knew how many times I almost called you…"

"I know you had to be respecting my wishes, Ian," she said. "Can you ever forgive me?"

"I already have."

"You…?" She backed away from him, eyes wide with wonder. "I don't deserve you."

"But you do. You deserve much more than you've already lived through, and I'm going to see that we make up for all the pain you've suffered."

She huffed out a breath, eyes going misty. "I love you. I missed you so much. And I'm going to make you so happy. Nothing's going to stop that."

Though he knew there was a lot to talk about, this blinding rush of giddiness, this dream-come-true of seeing her again triumphed over anything else. They would have a lot of time to work out Rachel's past, and he was the man to help her do it.

As the man who loved her, that was his job, after all.

Riding the moment, he took the small jewelry box out of his bag, and she covered her mouth with her hands. She was trembling.

He eased the hinges open. Nestled in a bed of black velvet, a diamond ring caught the dim light, flashing its brilliance over her skin, pinpoints of light and optimism.

"I bought this last night, praying you had called me here because you needed to be with me," he said. "I know we've gone so fast, but I love you, Rachel. I can't live, breathe, eat, exist correctly without you."

She laughed, taking her own velvet box out of her jeans pocket. Opening it, she exposed a golden band.

"Jinx," they both said, giving into their joy.

After they laughed and cuddled for a few minutes, Rachel held him to her, whispering in his ear.

"I love you, too," she said, "no matter how fast we've gone. But how long does it take to know that you've found the right person? The one who makes your day go so quickly because time isn't a fair player? The one who makes you think anything is possible?"

Ian melted right then and there. He was faintly aware that the bar patrons had gone silent.

"Marry me?" they both said at the same time.

They both burst out laughing again, so damned ecstatic to be together, just as if they were cooking omelets in her kitchen again, caught in an eternal afterglow that only got more intense by the hour.

Then they kissed, her tears salty on his lips as he took her in. She was back in his arms, a part of him, and he knew that from this moment forward, she would never leave again.

He'd never been more convinced of anything in his life.

Everyone in the bar applauded and hooted, encouraging Ian and Rachel. Unexpectedly, the flash of a camera interrupted them and, when Ian glanced over, he found Gilbert, grinning proudly, his own gaze hazy with beatitude.

Happiness at seeing his daughter find acceptance and unconditional love at last.

Gilbert pointed to the camera. "I thought this would be a good picture for all those nieces and nephews Rachel's told me about."

The best souvenir ever, Ian thought. Rachel. A gift his entire family was going to adore when he brought her home.

Keeping an arm around her, Ian moved forward to shake his future father-in-law's hand. Gilbert congratulated him, and so did Rachel's friends, who stepped out of the background now that the celebration had started.

Yes, tonight was for cheering, for heartfelt reunions and sorting out all the hard feelings that had kept Ian and Rachel apart.

But tomorrow…

Tomorrow would be Gilbert's day, Ian thought, giving his new fiancée another lingering kiss.

Because Alex Broadstreet was going to have his very own media circus.

The next evening's newscast showed the entire story.

Former president Alex Broadstreet waved off the cameras and reporters as he emerged from Saunders University's administration building. Students and detractors gathered around the man who had made a public mockery of their favorite teacher as flashbulbs went off.

The same female reporter who had covered Gilbert Harrison's trial spoke over the images of her subject. "Today, Alex Broadstreet was fired from his position of president of the college board of directors at Saunders University. According to a statement from the board, Broadstreet, quote, 'Shed a harsh light on school business by mistreating employees and misusing his position of power to harass faculty members.'"

As the screen showed Broadstreet struggling to get into his Lexus while reporters swarmed him, the reporter continued. "Almost one month ago, Broadstreet led the charge against Gilbert Harrison, a former professor here at Saunders. Many called the hearing 'illegal' and 'unethical.'"

Broadstreet managed to drive off in his car, his face contorted with what seemed to be anger mixed with impotence. To the casual viewer, he seemed to be driving in the opposite way of a sunset. In fact, when his car stuttered and stalled mere feet from the reporters, who chased him down again, a particularly openhearted observer might have felt pity for the man who seemed to be a prisoner of the media attention he'd so gleefully cultivated.

While the reporters wrapped up and signed off, the camera caught up to Broadstreet's driver's window, revealing the ex-president himself, who was covering his face with his hands.

Hiding himself from a taste of his own medicine.

Rachel and Ian were watching the report from her couch, his arm resting around her as she nestled against him. On their ring fingers, diamonds and gold sparkled as brightly as their promises.

They had talked the previous night away, made love during the day, ironing out all the wrinkles between them and planning for the future. They were going to get their own place here in Boston, where he could work on his job "from home" while taking a weekly investigative trip, and she would return to Nate's law firm, coming home to Ian's embrace.

They were going to start over, just as she had with Gilbert.

"Broadstreet's very own media circus," she said, running her fingers over Ian's chest. "I'm so sorry for accusing you of creating one for me. He was the real culprit."

Snow had settled outside, and a fire spread a glow throughout the room. When she glanced up at her fiancé—yes, her *fiancé*—his skin borrowed the orange hue from the flames, his gaze dancing with heat.

"I take my share of the blame. But, hell, it's not like that stopped me from selling *his* story. Poetic justice in motion."

"I sort of feel sorry for him."

"Broadstreet?"

Rachel huddled closer, resting her leg on Ian's lap, nestling her nose against his neck. Um. Warm, the scent of soap on skin. The scent of Ian, an essence she couldn't get enough of.

"Well, he's pitiful," she said. "I wasn't happy when Gilbert was down in the dumps, so it's hard to see another man in that position now—and very publicly, besides."

"What a sweetheart." Ian kissed her temple. "But he's getting his just deserts, Rachel. Don't waste another thought about it."

"You're right." She still felt crummy for feeling vindicated for Gilbert, though, even if karma had worked itself out. "But I think the best revenge is seeing Gilbert getting back on his feet. There's a spring in his step now that he's started work with the sports camp. That man was made to mentor kids."

"My audience is going to love him after his interview airs. You watch."

The fire snapped loudly, easing their conversation to silence. They'd already talked about tomorrow's interview thoroughly, and had also discussed their engagement.

Being a widow, Rachel advocated taking their time before they tied the knot. She knew that she had the rest of her life to savor each of Ian's nuances, to discover all of the surprising details about him. She also knew from experience that, no matter how in love you were, marriage could be a lot of work. So slow-driving sounded wise to her, because she trusted that they'd always be faithful, marriage license or not.

Trust. It was so easy with Ian.

Absently stroking circles on his belly, she said, "We're so lucky."

He shut off the TV by using the remote. The chatter of fire provided all the accompaniment they needed.

"Why?" he asked. "Because we both finally got our heads back together in enough time to save ourselves?"

There were so many reasons to count herself lucky, but the most important one was sitting right here, next to her.

"I hate to think of what might have happened if we'd both believed all my misgivings." Rachel crept her hand under his sweater, enjoying the feel of rock-hard abs and toasty skin. "I came so close to blowing it for us."

His breathing picked up. "You've come a long way. You've gained such strength, Rachel, and that's just one of the things I love about you."

Her heart basked under the light of his words. It wasn't ever going to close again. Ian had helped in teaching her to follow through, no matter how tough the circumstances.

She sat up, keeping her hand on his belly. "Know what? You're the best Christmas present ever."

Grinning, he gathered her in his arms, kissing her senseless, his lips moist, sucking and drawing at hers.

With a long *mmm,* she fell backward on the couch, taking him with her, pulling his sweater off with deliberate care.

Afterward, as he leaned on an elbow to look down at her, Rachel's body pounded in a dance, something primal, like a thanks to heaven for rain or sunshine or…Ian.

He used a thumb to flutter over her throat, then traveled a palm downward, increasing the pressure while he sketched a path between her breasts. Teasing her, he explored everywhere around them, stimulating her.

"You're wicked," she whispered.

Laughing, he traced his fingertips over one breast, brushing back and forth, no doubt knowing he had the luxury of taking it easy now that they'd promised themselves to each other.

"Hey," he said quietly, "I'm a reformed playboy, remember?"

"Honey." She pressed his hand over her, guiding him around and around her peaking nipple. "You can be as naughty as you want with me."

"I like the sound of that."

He bent his head, latched his mouth over her nipple, lightly gnawing at her. Even through the film of her bra and the cotton of her top, she could feel the wetness of his attentions.

Soon, he'd gotten her turtleneck and bra off, and she was bare beneath him, reveling in the slide of his chest against hers.

Her breasts were swollen with desire, sensitive to the slightest contact, burning as they met his skin. Rachel didn't know how she'd ever made it through life without Ian touching her, because his every move was engrained in her body, as if all her cells had been waiting for him to stir them up.

When he glided his hand downward, over her ribs, her tummy, and between her legs, Rachel moaned, never having realized before that she was so vocal during sex. With Ian, it seemed natural, a part of showing him how good he made her feel.

He lulled her to ecstasy with his hand, stroking her until she grew ready for him. Then he removed the rest of his clothing.

"I'm going to make you smile for the rest of the night," he said, returning to her and coaxing the jeans away from her hips, her legs.

Her satin underwear followed, thumping to the floor when he tossed them there. Soon, he was securing a condom over himself, increasing the anticipation of having him inside of her.

He leaned down, kissed her tummy, and Rachel bucked a little, involuntarily parting her legs while he slipped his lips down her skin. His tongue met the core of her, and she strained against every carnal kiss, every pull of his mouth.

Now her moans grew louder, increasing in tune as he loved her.

She dug her hands in his hair, flung a leg up on the couch's back, accommodating him, allowing him to make her smile all he wanted to.

While the room whirled around her, a silken layer of prickles wrapped around her skin, tingling, binding her to Ian. Her belly tightened, stretched, roared into itself like a mass of butterflies swirling together, flapping their wings inside, faster…faster…harder…

Just as she was about to flare open, Ian reared up and plunged into her. She met him with the churn of her hips, grasping him to her, urging him deeper.

She groaned, loudly…louder…

They felt as if they were spinning a cocoon around themselves, creating their own existence, making them one.

And as their passion built, whipping around and around to a climax, she clung to him, knowing her search for love was over.

But Ian wasn't a link in the string of her desperation. No, he was her strength, her soul, and she would stand firm by his side, bolstered by him.

Entwined with him.

He drove into her, faster, faster and then, with a cry of his own, he stiffened and spent himself.

She wasn't far behind.

The wings in her stomach spread through every limb, flittering and tickling, driving up the heat of her blood with sweet friction. Brushing, throbbing, beating with the rapid thrashing of a dying flock and…

…*there.*

As she got close to the sky, the fluttering stopped, allowing her to flow back down, catching the wind until she rested on the couch again, holding Ian as they both panted and came off of their highs.

It took a while before they had the breath to say anything. But when he was able to talk first, he made sure that she would indeed be smiling.

For more than the rest of the night, too.

"You're my biggest scoop, you know," he said.

"And a willing one."

With that, she folded into his love, knowing she was never going to seek another place to spend her days.

She'd never run from the shelter of his arms again.

Epilogue

They all gathered the next night at Gilbert's new home, a modest apartment near David and Sandra Westport's building. Ian Beck's interview had already wrapped up, and everyone had retired here in good cheer.

In fact, Gilbert was watching Cassidy and Eric decorating the Christmas tree that they had brought as a housewarming gift. She was simply glowing with the peace that Eric had given her with his love and his easing of her nightmarish past.

Gilbert gave thanks for the circumstances that had brought the couple together, in spite of what he himself had done to make everyone's year a little harder.

In a roundabout way, he believed he should even

force himself to be grateful for the trouble he had put everyone through, because this was the end result.

Love.

In one corner of the room, Sandra and David Westport hung stockings on a bookshelf, their once-faltering marriage strong and healthy.

On the couch, Nate Williams and Kathryn Price sipped from the same hot cider mug, having found inner beauty within the both of them.

Near the front door, Smith Parker was holding mistletoe over Jane Jackson's head, kissing her and giving her new hope in spite of all the disappointments they had suffered.

By the stereo system, Ella Gardner was teaching Jacob Weber all the words to the Chipmunks' Christmas song, and the one-time "bad boy" doctor was actually enjoying it while he sang the lyrics to Ella's ever-growing belly.

And, most touching, near the window, Ian Beck was embracing Rachel as they watched a new snow fall.

Gilbert had already accepted his future son-in-law wholeheartedly. Not only was Ian going to clear Gilbert's name on TV, showing him as the hero he had always intended to be, the reporter was going to take care of Gilbert's little girl, showering her with the love she had always craved and making her a more confident woman who could love him right back in the process.

When Cassidy called everyone around the tree, Gilbert stayed in his seat, unwilling to move, to destroy his perfect picture of the family he had accidentally put together.

But if he was pressed to tell the absolute truth, he might say that he didn't fit in with the joyful couples, anyway. That he was a lonely, anonymous face in the crowd yet again, the benefactor who had brought everyone happiness and didn't expect to be recognized for it.

He swallowed back the isolation and watched as everyone stood around the tree, with Eric lifting up Cassidy so she could place the star on top.

Yet before she could do so, Rachel glanced around, then found Gilbert sitting alone.

"Come on," she said, waving him over. "This is my first real Christmas. With my friends, my fiancé..." She smiled at him, and it lit up Gilbert's world.

"And my dad," she added.

For a full minute, he couldn't move. *Her dad.* Two words he had been waiting to hear forever, it seemed.

Even though he had made a lot of mistakes in his life, he had done many positive things, too, hadn't he?

And as his daughter, plus all the rest of the people he loved, welcomed him into their circle, he told himself that this was the best moment of his life.

That, in spite of all his errors, he had done some good after all.

* * * * *

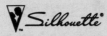
SPECIAL EDITION™

presents a new continuity

FAMILY BUSINESS

Bound by fate, members of a shattered family
renew their ties—and find a legacy of love.

On sale January 2006

PRODIGAL SON

by award-winning author

Susan Mallery

After his father's death, eldest son Jack Hanson
reluctantly assumed responsibility for the family
media business. But when the company faced
dire straits, Jack was forced to depend on
himself—and the skills of the one woman he
promised long ago he'd never fall for....

Don't miss this compelling story—only from
Silhouette Books.

Available at your favorite retail outlet.

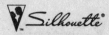

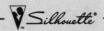

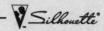

SPECIAL EDITION™

**The second story in
The Moorehouse Legacy!**

HIS COMFORT AND JOY
by Jessica Bird
January 2006

Sweet, small-town Joy Moorehouse knew
getting tangled up in fantasties about political
powerhouse Gray Bennett was ridiculous.

Until he noticed her…really noticed her.

**Alex Moorehouse's story will be
available April 2006.**

4 1/2 Stars, Top Pick!
"A romance of rare depth,
humor and sensuality."
—*Romantic Times* BOOKclub on
Beauty and the Black Sheep

Kate Austin makes
a captivating debut
in this luminous tale
of an unconventional
road trip…and one
woman's metamorphosis.

dragonflies AND dinosaurs
KATE AUSTIN

COMING NEXT MONTH

#1729 PRODIGAL SON—Susan Mallery
Family Business
After his father's death, it was up to eldest son Jack Hanson to save the troubled family business. Hiring his beautiful business school rival Samantha Edwards helped—her creative ideas worked wonders. But her unorthodox style rankled by-the-books Jack. They were headed for an office showdown…*and* falling for each other behind closed doors.

#1730 A PERFECT LIFE—Patricia Kay
Callie's Corner Café
The divorce was tough enough on Shawn Fletcher—selling the house and watching her ex remarry *really* stung. So a flirtation with her daughter's math teacher, Matt McFarland, came as a nice surprise. But when things with the younger man seemed serious, Shawn panicked—how would her daughter and the Callie's Corner Café gang take the news?

#1731 HIS MOTHER'S WEDDING—Judy Duarte
Private eye Rico Garcia blamed his cynicism about romance on his mom, who after four marriages had found a "soul mate"—again! Rico's help with the new wedding put him on a collision course with gorgeous, Pollyanna-ish wedding planner Molly Townsend. The attraction sizzled…but was it enough to melt the detective's world-weary veneer?

#1732 HIS COMFORT AND JOY—Jessica Bird
The Moorehouse Legacy
For dress designer Joy Moorehouse, July and August were the kindest months—when brash politico Gray Bennett summered in her hometown of Saranac. She innocently admired him from afar until things between them took a sudden turn. Soon work led Joy to Gray's Manhattan stomping ground…and passions escalated in a New York minute.

#1733 THE THREE-WAY MIRACLE—Karen Sandler
Devoted to managing the Rescued Hearts Riding School, Sara Rand kept men at arm's length, and volunteer building contractor Keith Delacroix was no exception. But then Sara and Keith had to join forces to find a missing student. Looking for the little girl made them reflect on loss and abuse in their pasts, and mutual attraction in the present….

#1734 THE DOCTOR'S SECRET CHILD—Kate Welsh
CEO Caroline Hopewell knew heartbreak. Her father had died, leaving her to raise his son by a second marriage, and the boy had a rare illness. Then Caroline discovered the truth: the child wasn't her father's. But the endearing attentions of the true dad, Dr. Trey Westerly, for his newfound child stirred Caroline's soul… giving her hope for the future.